Pangelicum

by Jim Marcus

December 2024

This book is set in Lato Regular 9/13
Titles in Lato Heavy 16/20

Cover:
Pangelicus
by Jim Marcus 2024

ISBN 979-8-9917282-9-4

WARNING

This book touches on the issue of suicide and
death which may be a cause of trauma for people
with suicidal ideation. If you or anyone you love
is dealing wth this issue, please reach out to the
Suicide Prevention Hotline at 998.

PULSEBLACK

Chapters

"A bird doesn't sing because it has an answer, it sings because it has a song."

--Joan Walsh Anglund

Forward: Four Words

By Sunil Aram

Probably the people who wrote the first Bible, the big one, wanted to add, in places, "Hey, please don't feed us to lions" but even back then they knew that this was a bad idea, historically, I think, mostly because it gives folks a suite of really folksy bad ideas and that's really regressive for everyone's general longevity.

The overarching message here is probably that if you want to live long enough to get hip replacement surgery and do daddy-daughter role play from the top, don't be a prophet. So, being super clear, this is not a bible, you aren't a prophet, it's all good, hope your hips hold out.

I'm typing this out on my phone's light-chain projector on the receptive countertop of the messy Capybara-themed cafe in Albina Suriname I found a few weeks ago in a drunken teleportation accident, so that should tamp down any lingering similarities between this narrative pigeonry and the bible handily. Mathew, Mark, Luke, and John weren't zotting off to South America after too much Malort to pet giant gerbils while drinking pricey chai.

If you love a good Capybara, though, and who doesn't, and your family trust has an extra thirty thousand dollars in teleport credits this week, I recommend it highly.

My family has money.

I can't really tell you how much because we're one of those families that consider talking about money to be really unpleasant and rude, but my grandfather invented the process whereby food can be readily 3d printed anywhere in the world with limited materials. This was a huge boon, helping to end world hunger everywhere except places where people couldn't afford it and were already really super fucking hungry. This is how capitalism works, ladies and gentleman, and, trust me, I've been working on it. Upending global capitalism is sort of a pet project of mine.

In the meantime, I have more money than I can ever spend, my health, a not insubstantial sized penis, and, up until a month ago, far too much time on my hands. If you're curious about that, I can start by telling you the shitty version of a story someone else told way better.

About a hundred years ago, in 1988, world famous author and involuntary AirBNB expert Salman Rushdie wrote his fourth book, a massive 547 page tome called "Satanic Verses." It was critically well received. Four stars all around on Amazon. Applause icons.

I read it. Which, given that my family is Muslim, is still a bit of a problem. Because he hadn't just written one of the finest pieces of storytelling in the English language, he'd inadvertently created a bit of enduring apostasy. People nowadays have their panties a little more ironed out but back then every panty hiding secretly under a muslim cleric's robe was heavily bunched.

Worldwide, various representatives of Islam began circling Rushdie like a massive kettle of flowing, dress-wearing bearded vultures. They didn't like how he'd portrayed the Prophet Mohammed in the book and they called for his death, which is a worst case scenario for an author, and totally undeserved, far worse than a thumbs down on goodreads. Speaking as someone who gave the teleport technician four stars even after he lost my socks and called me "overly girly", this is hard for my head to rotate around.

They even called for the death of the people at the publishing company, which is the kind of outrageous twenty-first century accountability that gun manufacturers have skirted for literally hundreds of years.

Well played, worldwide Islam.

Soon, the most famous man in a dress in the whole world, the Shah of Iran, The famed Ayatollah Khomeini, addressed a FATWA at him. In case you aren't an Islamic cleric, a fatwa is an irrevocable declaration of war on you, requiring that any good Muslim kill you on sight.

Rushdie had to go on the run. He had to hide. The kettle of vultures had turned into a wake of vultures, which is what they call a group of them when they are feeding together. I did not invent these words, so address your complaint letters accordingly. A group of angry letters is called a distribution of mail.

The next year, Khomeini died. Apparently, he was so disturbingly punctual that when he was a half hour late for dinner everyone just sort of wrote out their memorials, bought a black robe and gave up. No one even bothered to look for the body. And they were right. Dead late guy in a dress. I could be literally missing for a full year and people would just assume I was having bathroom issues.

But, before he died, while he did a lot of important quasi-mystical shit, he did not release the Fatwa. In fact, this is apparently what the word "irrevocable" means, as I see now perusing the dictionary.

No one can lift it.

"So Muslim leaders on Twitter called for his death. I didn't want to write that sentence, but there it is. Even the Romans didn't pull out their phones and take to twitter to call out Jesus. Insult to Injury, I think it's called. In case you aren't a student of history, Twitter was a social platform destroyed in the early twenty first century by a multibillionaire who got hair plugs, changed his name to "X" and got lost forever on a publicity space flight with Ted Nugent, A muppet, and some guy that ran a company called "My Pillow" that sold, like, just regular pillows.

I swear I researched that, but it still sounds nuts to me.

Salman Rushdie had to live on the run. Randos would just show up and stab him.

He wrote some brilliant stuff along the way, but the long and short of it was that he was persecuted by people who probably didn't even have an up-to-date library card.

And I'm not 100% sure they read the book.

Because the book is really good.

And it actually makes you LIKE the prophet Mohammed.

So, here is the story, paraphrased. The Caliph of the land calls Mohammed into his combination throne room/bowling alley. Mohammed has been going around telling everyone there is only one god- Allah. And people are buying it. They like his vibe. And one god is easier to remember, also a premium benefit to monogamy.

The Caliph, though, is concerned.

Way back over fifty years ago, in 2030, Hulu bought the rights and made this into a movie, so I'm going to just use the characters from the film.

The Caliph is played by Jonah Hill. A bit older and shaped more like Moneyball Jonah Hill, not thinner Jonah Hill from Wolf of Wall street or pudgy Accepted Jonah Hill.

Visualizing?

Ok. now here is where fatwas happen:

The Prophet Mohammed is played by Asif Mandvi, which I will never forgive for not giving us a fifth season of Evil, but the show goes on so here it is.

And the Calipha is played, for the purpose of this well received 2030's film, inscrutably turned into a rom com by Hulu higher ups, by Bella Haddid. Jonah really wants to make Bella happy.

Because how did that even happen? Damn. Good pull, Mr. Hill.

Now Jonah calls Asif into his bowling alley and he's like, "dude, my superhot wife is the head of the pagan church and she thinks there are a ton of gods. So, either you just tell us that yeah, some of her gods are ok. Or I have to smite you. You've got twenty minutes."

Again, I can't stress enough how much better a writer Salman Rushdie is than I am. In fact, go now, and read that book first, I'll wait. I'm just butchering this shit.

Done? Excellent.

So Asif Mandvi is a good guy. He's not in this to piss anyone off. He says, "ok, Ima going to go meditate and pray on this and i'll be back." And he does.

He goes off, in the film adaptation, which is sponsored by Hilton, to the Sheraton Medina and turns off all the lights and prays. He's there for only a couple hours before the angel Gibreel- Gabriel - shows up, in the film, played by a hilarious Sam Rockwell, well known for his performance in "Moon", and hands him some verse- some poetry, I guess. The prophet is like, "This is serious, man." and so Rockwell tells him that the verses just say, sure, buddy, you can tell him some of his gods are ok.

The prophet is so happy. He doesn't really know what smiting is, but he knows he wants no part of it. Basically, no problem with the Caliph. This is good news.

So Mandvi goes back to talk to Hill. They are both super happy and the Caliph gives him a house, a bunch of money, and some new shoes because it matters what you wear on your feet, prophet. No doubt.

And, for about three weeks, everyone is happy. Asif discovers he has a pool, which takes up like a week of that. Jonah and Bella make out in public a lot, which might not be super easy to watch, but everyone seemed happy. Then, one night, the prophet is in the hot tub, taking it easy, and the angel Gabriel shows up again, this time in a speedo, which, Not gonna lie, Sam Rockwell owned. He tells him that the last visit wasn't him - it was Satan. And those were Satanic verses.

So now, the prophet has to go back and tell Jonah that he was wrong. There is only one God and Bella is mistaken. The Caliph is not happy and tells him he's going to give him a day to run.

Asif packs up and runs. He's trying to stay alive, but he's still a nice guy so he's being careful about letting people know who he is or asking for help or anything. He engages in some shenanigans and hijinks because why not, it's a book. Have some fun, right? Then, eventually, he ends up in the pickle that earns the author the big Fatwa.

To get this, you have to know that the actual prophet, like the actual Jesus, were the kind of people with which you want to hang out, not the sticks-in-butts hyper judgmental prisses that religious people like to make them out to be. They both partied with everyone, washed some feet, defended fallen women, and generally forgave people with the cheerful rolling enthusiasm of a lifelong Canadian social worker.

The prophet ends up in a brothel. The ladies there think he's good people and they try to protect him. They pretend he's a eunuch and let him stay as long as he likes. No one thinks that the Prophet Mohammed is going to play act like a eunuch in a house of ill repute so people just walk right by him while he, eunuch-like, sings the high parts of various Hall and Oates' songs in flowy silk middle eastern MC Hammer pants.

This went over super badly and the entire Muslim world lost its shit. Even one of the executives at Hulu who greenlit the watered down version forty plus years later got a horrific lifetime ban from the local shawarma place while his secretary was beheaded.

I bring this up for a good reason. I'm trying to get to four little words. To me, these are four of the most important words in the world and in a second, you'll see why.

This entire story is evolving here in real time. It started at the dawn of time, I hear, but the part that involves me happened about a month ago where I became the new Angel Gabriel, the messenger of God.

It turns out that "Gabriel" isn't a name so much as it's a title, like "Door Dash Delivery guy" or "Therapist" and that title was inadvertently passed to me.

So the four words?

Don't. Kill. The. Messenger.

Seriously. It's my JOB to write this, not something I asked for. Just like my best friend, Gia, didn't ask to be Azrael, the new Angel of Death and my other best friend, Brooklyn, didn't ask to be Michael, the Avenging Angel.

This stuff apparently happens, and I never knew that, so caught up I've been petting giant floppy hamsters in South American cafe bookstores checking out Latin guys and learning how to say "Can I touch your chest" in spanish.

It's "¿Puedo tocar tu pecho?" in case you think I've been slacking. And, as a pickup line, it's really good.

As you read this, try to remember that.

Don't. Kill. The. Messenger.

Angels aren't that much different than you. And more like you now than ever. That's part of the story, really.

Are we perfect? No. Are we trying to be? Again, no, because that seems like a huge amount of uncompensated labor. But, like Sam Rockwell in a speedo, you can't always control the temperature in the pool but you can decide to dip down underwater and take a peek.

Or not.

But as I look back over the events of the past month, a lot is being made clear to me, things I might have missed when it happened. As I said, this is a job now, my job, basically, so i want to be a better narrator and help other people make sense of it all, before…

Well, mostly before people realize what's changed.

But the reality of the situation is bigger than all that. Luckily, I get to pick and choose what i reveal so that you don't have to sift through the nonsense to get to the important bits.

I hope you can walk out of this with a sort of mandate for how to live from now on in this new world. Throughout human history so many of the changes we've gone through have been gradual, delicate. Hell we can even pretend we don't notice. Every time, we might walk away with a little more power than before or a little less. We chalk it up to the whims of the universe and move on.

But I hope, after reading this, you come to the conclusion that there is a bigger arc to follow, one that creates its own kind of power. And with that would come the other thing, no denying.

But, like a lot of big ideas, both good and bad, It all started small. And that is all about proportion.

This one starts small with a couple of seats at the biggest, most expensive wedding you've ever seen.

The Wedding

"Did you invite your Tinder match to my Aunt's wedding for your first date? Please Advise" I leaned in, smoothly, to my phone like a spy.

Brook sat down with two drinks. "Watermelon Red Bull Vodka with lime." She and I were sitting on this side of the room and Gia looked like a little busty sparkly Bratz Doll over by the orchestra. She very clearly tried to avoid answering.

"She's not answering" I took a swig. Nothing watermelon flavored ever tastes like watermelon.

"Jesus, Sunny, this place is huge. How much money does your aunt have?" Brooklyn was a pretty Latina with dark eyes. She was wearing a slim white dress to someone else's wedding because of course she was. There was a plate full of appetizers in front of her and I slipped in and grabbed something that looked shrimpy."

"All the money. We don't talk about that in my family. But she was grandpa's favorite so let's just assume she can buy new bodies every week and will never ever die."

"She does look good."

I pressed the walkie talkie button on my phone. "I know you can hear me, you mostly silicon flavored bitch." From across the room Gia held up her hands and looked around, pretending she was hearing voices.

"She's ignoring me."

"This date is going to go insanely badly." of course it was. Who invites a tinder date to a wedding? Doesn't she have a Kia with a back seat? I thought that was funny so I said it out loud.

"Of course it is. Doesn't she have a Kia with a back seat?"

Brooklyn leaned too close to the phone and pushed the button. "It was your idea to be on walkie talkie mode so we can protect you. If you don't answer we're going to let you get raped and killed."

Gia responded. "You can't help, you're in a different zip code. No one can stop it." She shook her head under a mop of black curls.

"I know, bitch, this place is huuuuuge."

"Is Sunny there?"

"You can see me and you've been ignoring me. I'm literally waving right now."

"Or didn't he come?" From across the room, Gia laughed at me.

"Tell her I got her the rape and kill room for after her date. Fourteenth floor." I poured out some champagne. Have you ever poured alcohol out for someone that was so crazy expensive you couldn't help yourself from telling them? I took a seven thousand dollar sip from the Louis Roederer Cristal Brut 2070 and tried to figure out how to work the price into the conversation.

"Tell him I say thank you. We'll see how it goes." From across the room she waved her thirty five thousand dollar glass of champagne at me and I wondered if she knew. My uncle Rome bumped into her and she spilled it. I put my head down.

"Here." I passed the glass to Brook. "Here. Drink this."

"Thanks for letting us come, Sunny. I'm having fun." Brook was just out of a relationship with a girl I set her up with. So, this was penance, really.

But she was also my girl.

"You know you're my girl."

"You really want to tell me how expensive this is, don't you?"

"So bad, I do."

She laughed, "Ha. fess up. Come on."

"It's like seven thousand dollars a sip. You could buy Guernica with the bottles on every table here."

"Nice. I love that painting. I want to color it in."

"The eagle has landed. He is approaching." Gia's voice came from my phone like the intro of Charlie's Angels.

"The old guy?"

"That's my Uncle Ahmad."

"Don't you have like three uncle Ahmads?"

"I do, I can't tell the difference. There he is." I pointed to a thinly muscular pasty guy in a black suit with long sandy brownish hair. He was cute, in a recently released convict way. He wore no tie and his shirt was open to the third button. I have excellent vision, people say."

Brooklyn was thinking the same thing. "Ouh, is he just out of prison? Or a gigolo?"

Gia asked him how his prison stint went. He looked confused and explained that he worked as a dog groomer. We could hear everything they said but only she could hear us, with her ear plug in.

"I'm going to drink when you're wrong." I had another sip.

Well, you're about to go fucking liver dead, Armando, because I got nothing."

"He's kind of Ocean's Fifteeny" I thought out loud. The raping and killing should start soon, though, before I was too drunk to clean it all up.

"Ooh, ask him if he ever considered stealing one of the dogs?"

"Is this like a Bladerunner human-or-robot quiz?"

"I would steal the dogs if the owners sucked."

He took his jacket off. You can't take your jacket off at a wedding before you've been there at least an hour.

"Gia, is he going to strip down completely? Let us know. Over"

"I don't think you have to say that. Sun."

"It's walkie talkie mode. Ok. Tell him I'll give him twenty thousand dollars to take off his shirt."

"How cum you never gave me twenty thousand dollars to take off my shirt?"

"You do that for free. Besides, I once gave you thirty thousand for a motorcycle with a sidecar so you could pretend to be in a lesbian knitting gang."

"Stich Bitches, yes, good times."

From across the room we could see him stand up and unbutton his shirt.

"It's coming off."

We jumped up and cheered. I took a big drink. As he sat back down, shirtless.

"He looks good."

"Almost Ocean's Sixteen."

At that moment, the ceiling lit up in stars. All of it was one giant light bank. And my Aunt Dimah was the main event.

Her face filled the screen, hundreds of feet wide. And at her side was Hamza, her partner for the last year or so. He owned a string of Hotels across the west coast. She owned the west coast. It seemed like a good union. For future reference, no one should ever have their face blown up thousands of times their rightful size. Dimah's left nostril floated ominously over our heads like the death star. It wasn't not terrifying.

In the center of the room, a fifty foot tall hologram showed Quadir, the Imam. For people into old cinema, it sort of conjured up an Islamic Star Wars Vibe. I tried to lean into that. If they really wanted to make this work, they could have gotten lightsabers at every table.

"Help me, Obi-Wan."

"Right?"

"If you spend this much on a wedding, you pretty much HAVE to stay together, don't you?"

"That's the idea, I think." I would personally be embarrassed to get a divorce after all this. Sorry. We just decided on the honeymoon we don't like how the other one smells. Do Over?

"Ok, I'm bored with Tinder Girl. Unless she literally gets lucky on the table, she's got nothing."

"How about that guy?" I pointed to a giant black man I'd never seen before with dreads and tattoos everywhere.

"Is that black Aquaman?"

"I think he's not wearing any shoes."

"Rock the vibe, Black Aquaman." Brook took another sip. Maybe ten thousand dollars worth?

"There's more of them. Weird." I pointed. There were two other people walking toward the center of the room. Each dark as night, stuffed into a suit, with long messy dreads, filled with metal and jewels.

"Holy shit." Brook saw them. "Are these people related to you?"

"Look at me. Look at these people. They're like superheroes. I'm a Jimmy Olsen Body Double. "

"What are they doing?" Brooklyn stood up to see.

And that's when it all went to shit.

One of the Black Aquamen put his left hand on a table and threw it behind him. In seconds, the entire room was up, running from the center tables, trying to reach the doors. No one wanted to see what was happening.

One or two other people were rushing to help. A familiar-looking tall man with green eyes and a purple jacket put his arm on the man's shoulder.

And it was ripped off.

I understand, I do. Nobody likes weird shit. But this was my family's wedding. I started moving toward the table. The biggest man, let's call him Black Mamba, reached toward a woman sitting at the table - a quiet looking black woman with short dark hair in a dark green dress. He put his hand around her throat.

And he lifted her off the ground.

Sonofabith. I yelled out "Hey. What are you doing?"

Brooklyn was right behind me. "I think he's strangling her. STOP IT."

Holy shit. "They weren't stopping for anything. The woman in the green dress seemed to be the center of their attention, with all three converging on her. Her head was falling sideways at an odd angle as he held her over his head. I was afraid that he might have already killed her.

Suddenly, a shirtless man hit him from the side, knocking him over. It was Giana's date. And she was right behind him, holding her burgundy dress, running to the woman. I dropped to my knees next to her. The woman didn't look good.

"Watermelon Red Bull. Damn. Gia, is she alive?" Brooklyn seemed to recognize her.

"Yep. I don't know how. I think her neck is broken."

"I made a motion to get up, "There's two more guys"

"She held me down, "Stay. You have to keep her head straight." She started chest compressions while Brookly and I struggled to keep her straight and block her from the men.

A couple of other men had advanced on the three men, including my uncle Hanif but they weren't doing well. A blondish girl was huddling under the table. I could see she wanted to come to the woman's aid, but she looked terrified. And like most everyone else there, maybe a little drunk.

Brooklyn stood up and screamed. The three men looked at her. I'd never seen eyes so alien and strange. "She's dead. You better get the fuck out of here."

They looked down at the woman in the green dress. She wasn't moving.

The first one pushed Gia's date to the ground and stood up to his full height.

I'll never forget what they did next. All three of them raised their arms and yelled out a few syllables in a language I'd never heard before.

כרדסן〉ᓑ ᔭᐧᑭᐧᑭᒥᑐᑕᑌᐧᑎ ᒋ ᒐᐧᒥ〉ᔭᐧᑎᑐᑯᓄ 'ᑭᐧᒣᑐ ᒐ᙮ᔭ ,ᐸ

And a storm of bluish fire surrounded them, seemingly atomizing them completely.

I fell backward, covering Gia's date, who was still on the ground. "Steven, Watch out"

"What the fuck?" Brooklyn stood there with her mouth open.

"Are they gone?" Gia Held her position over the woman's body. People were rushing in to assist now.

"She's alive. I don't know how." She looked over at her date, still shirtless. "Steven, help me get her up while they hold her head. I don't know how it's still attached."

He picked her up and we made our way to the doors.

I thought. "This is how you get out of a wedding in style."

"Why do people say they don't like hospitals? What could there be to like about hospitals? It's not like people are running around throwing parties in hospitals." I think I really wanted to know.

"I didn't hate them. When I was a paramedic the people were cool to me. It was like another place you could go where people liked you." I had forgotten that Gia used to be a paramedic until I saw her working on that woman in the green dress. It's funny what you forget.

"Yes, they liked you, because they were putting you to work." Brooklyn took a swig, "Crack that fucking whip." She had another bottle in the other hand. She could have bought a whole wing in this hospital if she'd stolen one more.

"Yeah, but it was just saving people." She got artificially serious, "Ms. Cooper, I don't mind coming out, but don't you remember what we discussed? If the base has flare, put it right up there."

I liked that. "That is catchy."

"We need some service around here." Brooklyn stood up and moved toward the nurse's station. She yelled out, "Ok, Nursies, it's time to come clean."

Gia jumped up to calm her, "Shh. sh. Do not yell in the hospital."

"I have special needs."

"No, you don't sweetheart. You're just drunk." Gia pet her on the arm.

Giana's date walked around the corner, still topless, "ok, guys, she's fine. Somehow, she's just bruised. They won't tell me more until you give me my shirt back."

"I don't think that's true." She tossed him his shirt.

I looked him over, "Well, I'm glad you're ok, Steven."

He sighed, "Thanks for the cover. What's your name?"

I held out my hand. "Oh, I'm Sunil. It was my obnoxious family."

"Well. Thank you for the invite. I'm going to go now."

Gia looked confused, "You're going?"

"Yes."

"How cum?"

"It's been an eventful night."

"Ok."

"But mostly because she called me an idiot." He looked at Giana.

She scrunched her face up. Her skin was so dark and perfect.

"I'm sure she didn't mean it."

"And, no offense, Man, All of you, but my name is Tim."

I thought. Was it? "Is it? Are you sure?"

Steven let out an exhausted breath and slid his shirt over his shoulders. He turned and walked away.

Gia put her arm around my shoulder. "I thought it was Steven, too."

"You're a terrible first date."

"You guys were supposed to help me. That's why we had the phone on."

Brooklyn handed her the bottle, "We're single too, babes."

"I knew that. Still, I hoped."

A young nurse walked by. She looked like she might have been Chinese or Korean with dyed blonde streaks in her hair. Gia looked up, "Excuse me. I think her name is Emma. She's in 214. We're the ones who tried to help her at the banquet hall. Can we see her?"

"She doesn't want to see anyone." The nurse looked around and then back at us, conspiratorially, "She's on suicide watch."

I pointed to Brooklyn, "She's been on suicide watch since High School."

"It really works." Brook took another drink.

The nurse stared, "You can't drink in here."

"Ballsy thing to say to someone on suicide watch."

In my head, all I could think was, "well, that's why people don't like hospitals."

I figured it was a good night for the girls to stay by me. Honestly, I figured they'd be too drunk to get home anyway, so I planned for it. Back at the hotel, we stepped off the Elevator on the floor right before the roof. It was white and antiseptic.

"So we're spending almost a hundred grand to get home for the night?" Gia looked around.

"Think of it as a well earned vacation after today. You guys have teleported with me before." I tried to remember how many times.

"Yeah, but where are we going?" Brooklyn was the drunkest of us all. One bottle was empty but she continued to carry it for balance.

"I have a place In Tonga. It's pretty cool. We can sober up and forget about tonight."

Gia looked at me, "Isn't that a whole bunch of islands?"

"Yep. My family has one. Near Tongatapu."

"Just one?"

The teleporter was at the end of the hall. It was clean, pristine, every inch of it white. Gia laughed.

"You know we should totally cover this thing in blood for the next people who use it. That's an art project. They'll be like, "I don't know, guys.""

"And like some little chunks of meat."

"And a pair of soiled underwear. People are terrified of appearing naked."

That was fun.

Brook put one of the bottles in a receptacle next to the machine. "What do we know about this Tonga place?"

I stepped up. "Well. It has one of the biggest underwater volcanoes in the world."

"Will that be coincidentally erupting this weekend? Because shit is going down all over."

"Likely not. Another chug or two and you will be."

"One of us should, island boy."

I held her arm and we entered. The ad wall lit up alerting us to the beautiful weather in Bermuda. I made a mental note for next time.

I pressed my wrist against the dashboard and typed in coordinates on the pad next to it.

"Ready."

"Have you ever seen that Fly movie?" Brooklyn tossed the bottle.

I sighed and pressed enter. "He was really giving Steven"

I found Gia on the beach the next morning, naked, spinelessly reclining on her back, on an adjustable beach chair about 200 feet from the first wave. Her skin looked impossibly dark against the white sand all around us. The 10am sun was positioned nearly right above us but it wasn't as hot as I thought it would be.

"I'd get naked, too, but I'd be a baked potato in twenty minutes."

"Why do white people have beach houses if they fear the sun?"

"Well, I'm light brown, but I can't tell you why anyone in my family does anything. I've been trying to figure that out for 20 years."

"It's so nice here. I honestly don't know why you ever come back."

"You can stay here and work. You're an artist, you can work from anywhere."

"Yeah, but art requires pain and I don't see any of that here. Unless you brought some with?"

"Nope. I made a point not to."

We sat in silence in the sun, listening to the beach sounds for about twenty minutes. I did have one question, but it could wait.

"I didn't handle that very well, did I?" she asked without looking.

"The rescue? Hell yes, you did. That woman would be dead without you. You're a fucking superstar."

"I think I meant the date."

"Ah. Yes. Well."

"I did call him an idiot. I was just playing around."

"I'm sure. I think I owe him twenty thousand dollars."

"Ten."

"Hm?"

"I told him he'd get ten thousand to take off his shirt. Then he did. I told him he'd get another ten to take off his pants. He said no and I..."

"Called him an idiot"

"Yep."

"What's that way?"

"That way is back home. New York almost the other side of the world? Why?"

"Does that look familiar?"

I followed her finger, pointing. In the distance I could see a column rising into the sky, made of what looked like the same blue flames that the men at the wedding had disappeared into. The column was half a planet away and only saw it because we were on the empty side of that planet.

But it was there.

"What the fuck is that? And who were those people at the wedding?"

I stood up and started taking pictures with my phone.

"I have no fucking idea."

The Wedding (Yes, I know)

Emma Jackson was dying in what would have been a beautiful hotel room if it had only been tidied up a bit.

About an hour earlier, she had found a thick purple rope in the top drawer of the west facing armoeire, left behind, no doubt, by the sexually adventurous couple, married fastidiously to other people, that had stayed here in room 515 and paid nearly twice as much as the initial booking rate for a late 3PM checkout time, wrapped one side around her neck and the other around the thick Austrian-Bavarian beams that spread across the ceiling of the room, stepped onto a chair, kicked it out, and hung herself.

The beams were only for show. Despite being very strong, they weren't needed for the structural integrity of the room. That was one thing they don't tell you at this very expensive, high class hotel.

One of the other things they don't tell you about is that in the case of a VERY late checkout, a maid will be required to clean the room in fifteen minutes or less, compressing the usual time taken to clean a full suite by a factor of four, with no additional pay.

The third thing of interest in this room right now was likely the fact that all of this had happened an hour ago and Emma Jackson, still dressed in her powder blue maid uniform, had been hanging by the neck the entire intervening time and was was still kicking, sputtering, gagging, choking, and very much alive.

Her eyes were open as she heard the knock on the door. She tried to spin herself in the direction of the knock.

"Hello. Anyone in there? Are we good to book the room?"

The doorknob shook slightly. Not rudely, never rudely. This was a very expensive hotel, as we discussed above. All efforts were taken to make sure that the idiosyncrasies of their wealthy patrons were accounted for.

Emma Jackson tried to yell out. At this point, her throat had closed up from trauma nearly completely. Ischemia to her brain due to physical compression of her carotid and vertebral arteries, along with a constantly breaking hyoid bone rendered her yells muffled and unintelligible.

The man behind the door shook the knob one more time. Emma could see, even at this distance, that the interior lock was set. She closed her eyes.

When she reopened them, the blueish-black skinned man was still there, seated on the couch in a long expressive robe. His skin was covered in tattoos and scars, marks and strange drawings, a language that she was unfamiliar with. She felt her brain dying from lack of oxygen again and made herself still for a minute until it turned back on again.

When she looked out again he was still there.

"He probably thought they were still in here fucking."

Emma screamed again. There was barely a sound.

"This is exhausting for me. I don't know what it's like for you, Emma. Are you ready to talk?"

After an hour of dying and coming back, Emma was ready to talk and shook her head. She still wasn't buying any of this, though.

The blue skinned man waved his finger, as slightly as it was possible. And Ema fell to the floor, holding on to her neck. Emma was a shorter woman, barely five foot tall. You couldn't call her fat, although kids often did walking to the lifts in this fancy neighborhood. She was curvy.

Her friends considered her cute.In an interesting coincidence that means nothing, having been born in 2050, she was exactly twenty years older than the seven dollars a sip Louis Roederer Cristal Brut 2070 drunk at the wedding she would soon be in attendance at, making her 38 years old. In all honesty, she was a smart, funny, complex and interesting woman with a, not going to lie, banging butt, who should have been anywhere but here, dying on the floor of a hotel room she hadn't had the chance to clean yet in her powder blue maid uniform.

The man was tall, but it seemed to mostly be in his legs. He was dark and powerful looking and his robe was completely spotless, a difficult task for any article of clothing at four in the afternoon, Emma thought.

But you would expect that from God.

He leaned back on the couch and pulled out a piece of paper. "While you're recovering your ability to speak, I wanted to run this past you - to see if it sounded familiar:

"And every little thing

would be how it should

And every little star

would want somebody good

Then you could be happy,

Because I could be wise

Free from the torture,

Free from the lies

I'd wait til the morning,

when daylight revealed

The covenant hope

The contract resealed

If I were God

This time."

"Is that how the song goes?" he folded the paper and slid it into his robe pocket.

Emma rubbed her throat and felt her ability to speak returning. She answered quietly.

"I think the Chorus repeats twice, actually."

The man pursed his lips. Emma considered for a minute that this may well explain what was wrong with the universe. That this person in front of her, ostensibly God, had no real sense of humor.

"Except I do have a sense of humor. Be terrified. And, yes, I know what's in the hearts of man. Even Santa Claus kind of knows what people are thinking."

He moved over to her and squatted down in front of her. Emma couldn't help but think, even after dying for an hour, that he was less impressive than she thought he might be. She thought that loudly.

"We could go back and forth with you psychically insulting me or we can deal. Which do you want?

"Why can't you leave me alone?"

"This is how the rules work."

"What rules?"

"Ok," God walked over to the bar and picked up a glass. He filled it with water and lifted it.

The water became gold and cloudy and a lemon appeared. He handed it to her.

Emma took the glass and looked at it.

"It's a lemon drop. At least I think it is. I literally haven't made a drink for anyone in 400,000 years."

Emma took a sip and moved to the couch to sit down. "It's pretty good."

"Oh, fuck you. It's your favorite. And it's great."

"Are you going to watch me die for a few more hours after this, because if so, I'll nurse it."

"That was no fun for me. Not to sound like a ten year old but you started it. Tell me, why were you trying to kill yourself?"

"You know what's in my heart, you tell me."

"This conversation is going to get really one sided. But here we go. Kai. He was only five, right? You had him when you were thirty two. Leukemia. I know it's been a hard year. You feel these things so...powerfully."

"These things? Children dying?"

"Yes." He walked back to the bar. "When I was younger, before all this, we would get drunk our own way."

He held up a glass full of a clumpy white liquid. "Mammoth milk. You have to leave it sitting around a bit."

He chewed up some stalks and spat them in the glass, "Oats and hops. You chew them up to release what's inside. The spit helps, too."

"A tiny bit of honey. If the mammoth doesn't kill you, the bees will."

He held up the glass and held his hand over it. "Let it ferment. For months. Crush it, filter it."

Now the liquid in the glass was watery and slightly milky, a little brownish yellow.

"Then you drink it." He downed the glass. He made a face.

"And every time, it was just terrible. But if you did it right, you were drunk. And you could make it one more day."

Emma raised her glass. "Well. THAT I know about." She took a long chug off the drink in her hand.

God moved over to the other side of the couch. He sat facing her. "Do you want to hear a story?"

"Will you go if I do?"

"Probably not. Who knows. I move in mysterious ways. But it's a good story. It beats choking to death all night. Most things do."

Emma forced a slight nod and took another drink. She lifted it up and watched it refill itself. That wasn't a bad trick. She could make some money with a glass like this.

Almost half a millennium ago, I woke up cursing. There was a plague killing off all my people. They probably don't mention in anthropology class much of this. Once there were nine races of man. My particular race Homo Rhodesiensis was not destined to survive. Some anthropologists call us Rhodesian man. Our line was a dead end. And much of it was because we had a pretty shit immune system. That turned out to be more important than anyone thought, by the way. Spoiler. "

"I lost four children before they were the age of five. Seven altogether. I really thought one would survive. Goro was so strong. He was a beautiful child. And oh, he was so good at everything. People didn't realize he was funny. So funny. He didn't need to be, you know. He was strong and handsome. I figured he'd outlive me. He did not."

"I'm sorry."

"I know. This part probably sounds familiar."

"Couldn't you stop it, with all your power?"

"Well, that's what I'm telling you. At the time I wasn't God. Someone else was."

"How is that possible?"

"It's actually how it works. I've been God for virtually the entirety of human history. The only god men on this planet have known. But there was one before me.

"The original God?"

"No. But it had been around for a few million years. Unchallenged. There was one before him. The rules always work the same."

"What rules?"

"I've been God for over 400,000 years. However, in their heart, If someone really wants the job, and they meet a few criteria, they can challenge me. I challenged him. I wanted it more than he did."

"Challenge God to BE God?"

"Yes."

"And when I sang that song I wrote at the open mic last week, THAT was a challenge?"

"It was. A good one. So," He leaned forward and she could see that the arcane markings were even on his teeth.

"So I'm here. And I just want to know. Do you want the job?"

Zeriakl sat down in the flimsy hotel chair at one end of the table one over from table 200. Kire and Nondukoma sat across from him. The table seemed almost cartoonishly short as did the Waiter who approached them.

"Hey, I'm Emad. I didn't know this was a table until a few minutes ago, so I'm sorry you have no silverware. Are you with the Bride's side or the Groom's?"

Zeriakl looked at him. Despite the fact that he was sitting down, his head was still a good four inches higher.

"Both."

"Oh, excellent, that sounds like a fun story. Are you guys going to want the chicken or the Lamb?"

The other two men nodded at Zeriakl.

"Both."

"Oh. ok. Hungry, yes, I get it. I'm going to get you silverware and plates and we'll get this show on the road. Is that ok?"

All three men nodded. Their blue-black skin, massive frames and long black dreads, peppered with beads and charms shook as they laughed affably."

Emad thought, for a moment, about his "show on the road" euphemism and decided it must be a lot funnier than he had originally thought.

Nice table, though. Good people. Looked kind of like a dark Jason Momoa from Aquaman. He placed the drinks in front of them, leaving a few extra. These guys sort of looked like they could drink.

Zeriakl lifted the drink to his mouth. "I deny God and all his works and consider myself to be derelict, fallen, debased, and no longer affiliated with the one true God." He took a big sip. The other two looked on in awe. He put the drink down and sat there for a second.

"Do you feel any different?" Kire fingered his own glass.

"Not yet. I'm waiting."

"Maybe you have to drink the whole thing." Nondukoma lifted his. "I deny God and all his works and consider myself to be derelict, fallen, debased, and no longer affiliated with the one true God". Then he drank it down with one gulp, tossing the glass across the room where it shattered against the far wall.

"That is not very discrete." Zeriakl said, downing the rest of his glass.

"To Rebellion," Kire lifted his glass. "I deny God and all his works and consider myself to be derelict, fallen, debased, and no longer affiliated with the one true God." Then he poured it down his own throat. He made a motion to toss the glass aside, thought better of it, and put it back down on the table.

"Today, we are fallen," Nondukoma said proudly.

Kire looked across the table, "I don't really FEEL fallen."

Zeriakl grabbed another drink, "It's just a drink. All of this is symbolic, really. Just how the rules work."

"Is she going to be here?" Kire looked around, grabbing another drink. It had been almost half a millennium since he'd had a drink. That being said, it wasn't terrible, just more carbonated than he'd anticipated. The bubbles tickled his nose.

"He's meeting with her now."

"When he does it, will we feel it?" Nondukoma asked delicately. Zeriakl was really no older, but it was his place to lead. Nondukoma scratched his back, where his great black wings met his shoulder blades. He didn't mind the suit, but if it came without sleeves, that would have been optimal.

"I just don't know. We're in new territory. We're now fallen, in open rebellion, so we will survive this transfer of power. Then, we begin the challenges. And, eventually, we take over."

Zeriakl looked around. He stared razor blades into the very soul of a passing waiter. He hadn't eaten either in over four hundred thousand years. Maybe some rice would be nice. Or one of those little meatballs.

"Fuck God." Kire yelled. The young couple over at the other table clearly only half heard him as they raised their glass to him and smiled. He drank and smiled back with a wide mouth full of deadly white sharpened teeth.

Zeriakle and Nondukoma looked over at him. Kire looked thoughtful. Maybe cursing out loud would make him feel more fallen. It did not.

"Taking the lord's name in vain? Nice."

"It's not helping."

"There's a shitload of other commandments to choose from. You can covet some asses on the way out of here, after we take out this new God." Zeriakle seemed so confident.

Nondukoma looked sad. "I'll never be the Uriel again." He lifted his glass, "to enlightening humanity with divine knowledge." He poured one out.

"Here, here," Zeriakl took another drink. "When this new god arrived, they would have a window to take her out before she got comfortable in her power. If he was drunk enough not to remember killing her, that would be nice. This was a long way from being the angel of inspiration.

Emad arrived with a few plates of appetizers. He slid a whole plate down on the table for them, winking. He kicked up a leg and moved on to the next table.

"I think he likes you."

"I could probably fuck some commandments up with him."

Nondukoma lifted his glass, "To tearing the ass off some commandments."

"Woo," the other two klinked glasses as they started devouring the appetizers.

Kire looked hypnotized. "Hail Satan, these fucking little shrimp things are worth losing your soul over."

"Do you see her?" Nondukoma swallowed a few meatballs whole. It was the sauce that did it. Like a red sauce but with just a tiny bit of curry in it. It mattered.

Zeriakl closed his eyes. As the Jeremiel, he could see the future. He knew. He'd foreseen all this weeks ago. But right now, it all looked so hazy, as if everything were in flux. There was no way to know. He saw one thing.

"I see the color green."

The other two tried to look impressed. They were not. It wasn't exactly Nostrodamus.

"We can play I spy with my little eye all night, but she'll be here." Kire shoved two more appetizers in his mouth, including the mini paella on a socarrat cracker. That was inspired. He thought for a moment about his place as Raguel and how it had been part of him for hundreds of thousands of years.

Everything was going to be different. He knew. There was no going back now.

Zeriakl pointed to the entrance where Emma walked in, in a pretty dark green dress. She had a shall around her shoulders and no purse. "And there she is."

"Wait, that's her?" Kire looked closely. She seemed harmless. Somewhere between 35 and 40, quiet, even thoughtful. She looked around the room as though she didn't belong there.

Nondukoma stood up. "Are you sure?" He was nervous. All of this was happening so quickly.

Emma glided her way to the center of the room and sat in an empty chair. A presentation began, playing across the ceiling, and she looked up.

Most everyone looked up. "Here we go." and Zeriakl got up and began walking. He stepped briskly toward her. The other two got up and followed.

With his enormously long legs, it took him no time at all to reach the center of the room, a room that descended into chaos very quickly after he grabbed the table and threw it against the far wall.

Zeriakl lifted the woman in the green dress off the ground and crushed her windpipe. It took almost no effort. The skin of her neck felt soft and pliable and crushed under his fist easily as her head lolled backward.

The three of them fought off the stragglers, wedding party guests that hadn't run off. Then, a dark haired woman stood up and yelled at him, imploring him to leave the woman alone.

She said she was dead.

The three of them looked at each other as they raised their arms. In perfect Syriac, Zeriakl recited to the sky the words they had used for millennia, "We beg you, Bring us home."

The familiar blue fire enveloped them and the room began to fade. Nondukoma was the first to think, as their surroundings faded, That this may have been a mistake. He, Kire, and Zeriakle were now fallen, no longer members of the Angelic army.

So where, exactly, was home now?

The Heroes of Tonga

Brooklyn had been screaming for a full minute when I got to her room. People are going to judge and ask questions later so I'm going to come clean.

Yes, I peed first. I heard her yelling and dove out of bed, got to the door and it just hit me. I had to pee. And I knew that if I showed up in her room and couldn't stop what she was yelling about because I was dancing around trying to keep my legs closed it would reflect badly on me so I quickly peed. In my defense, though, I did that thing where you only pee to sort of "top off" your bladder and get back to it, knowing you'll have the chance later.

So when I showed up in her room, Gia was already there and I wasn't 100% sure I didn't still have to pee a little more. If anyone ever makes a movie out of this, can you leave this part out?

Definitely put this part in, though. Brookly was wrapped in a blanket, hovering about three feet off above the bed. She was yelling and complaining. Gia had her head cocked and was staring at her.

"So, that's a fucking thing, huh?" She said, without looking at me.

"What the fuck, Brooklyn."

She stopped yelling for a minute. "Can you see under this? I'm not wearing underwear."

I looked down. I was wearing my Tuesday pajamas. "So, you're just free-balling in my guest bed."

Giana turned to me, "I think, when women do it, it's called free flapping."

Brooklyn made a face of disgust. "Oh, I don't like that at all."

"Tell it to merriam-websters." Gia's voice dropped as she asked me, "No biggie, but is this, like, the Penn and Teller room? Is this shit normal?"

"No, this is some Chriss Angel Mindfuck shit."

Gia looked up. "Hey, babe. Dunno if this is safe."

I tried something, "You need to come down. Down, now."

"I'm not a dog, Sunil."

"That's fair."

"Why is this happening?"

"There's like nothing underneath me at all. I think this is a miracle. I think you should call the church."

"I'm a muslim, I don't have the church's direct line."

"Do mosques do exorcisms?" Gia really seemed to want to know and I didn't.

I stepped over to the other side of her and it was true. She WASN'T wearing panties. And she was just floating there. It was wild. "Can you control this? Could you float up if you wanted?"

"I'm not sure. I haven't really been trying, I was just freaking out." She arranged the covers around her and slid silently another foot or so upward.

Gia and I were entranced, "Oh, my Jesus, that is fucked up."

"You're flying." I realized now that this was the proper terminology."

Gia waved her hand under her and then tweaked her exposed butt. "This is really real. Holy shit."

We'd been on this island doing absolutely nothing for over a week and now, out of nowhere, Brook was supergirl.

"Girl, You're supergirl."

"I am totally supergirl."

"Fly to the right now." Gia clapped her hands together.

Brook moved a few feet to the right. Her right.

"Close enough. Now fly into the kitchen and get me Mexican Pepsi."

"I'm a super hero, not your super bitch, get it yourself."

Gia looked at me, "She's the same, just more floaty."

"Have you ever done this before?" It seemed like a reasonable question.

"Sun. If I spent the weekends flying around Manhattan, don't you think I would have mentioned it in one of our three hour bathtub phone calls?"

"Yes. ok. What do we do?"

"We make a note and then move on. Do you guys think this has anything to do with the Jason Momoas? I mean, she yells at them, they disappear in magic blue flame, she flies?" Gia wrapped her robe around herself and pulled out her phone, scratching her butt on the way to the kitchen.

Research time.

The automated kitchen was already in the middle of making breakfast. The breakfast buffet print attachment was an additional add-on for food printers that sold for almost forty thousand dollars wholesale. It was a recent favorite for chain restaurants who received a quality bump for their management of breakfast, which was most of them.

It's why they did it.

Think about it. No one at Wendy's wanted to start serving breakfast. But the public perception, once they started doing it, was, "hey, there's an egg in this thing, these motherfuckers must be grownups." And then they bought a square hamburger later, thinking everybody had their shit together.

Gia had set her phone on the table. Blue laser lines shot out and built a keyboard and display across the center of the table. I put my phone across from hers and it automatically integrated. The display wrapped the whole table. Brook padded in behind us eating a banana. She had made it back to the ground, apparently.

And now, she made her way to the table where the two of us were absorbed in the screens. A tiny buzz went off.

Breakfast was ready.

"I'm back on the ground, if anyone cares."

Gia found it first. "Hey, apparently, three days ago, New York got its first superhero."

I heaped some hashbrowns on my plate. The crispy kind. "Hey, I thought I was New York's first superhero."

Brook took my plate and sat down. "Not counting Supergay, the man of silk."

"Still not an insult." I started making another plate.

"Her name is Veridian and she can fly, make plants grow, and heal people."

"That sounds gayer than Supergay."

"Is there a picture?" Gia reached up her hand and I put the plate in it. Third time's a charm.

A picture of Veridian appeared as a hologram in the center of the table. She was flying, spinning around her center mass.

She kind of looked familiar.

"Shit. Do you think this is the era of superheroes?" Brook tried to touch the hologram. It's 2088 and some people still try to touch holograms.

"Can you heal and grow plants, too?" That was a sentence I never thought I would say. And it made her step back a bit.

"Do you want me to heal your spine?"

"For the last time, I don't have curvature of the spine. I just hunch."

Gia stood up and put a bunch of Bacon in her robe pocket. "Let's go run some tests."

"Are you guys my sidekicks now?" Brooklyn ran out to the enclosed yard. It was huge and you could see a number of bedrooms flanking it. This place was ostentatious, to be sure. Her black hair looked almost blue in the sunlight. The red undertones in Gia's hair were obvious here, too. I wondered how much color the Tonga sun could tease out of us.

"Fuck no." It would be hard to Imagine Giana being anyone's sidekick. I was forced, however, to now consider some hard truths about myself.

"I think I'm already HER sidekick."

Gia didn't miss a beat. "He is. And I'll fight you for him."

"Well, that would make you a supervillain by default, because I am a superhero." Brooklyn raised her hands up to shoulder level and lifted about a foot off the ground.

We applauded.

"Look at that fine control."

"Without a cape, I don't buy it. It's not true flying, it's just fucking around in the air."

"Wait," Gia did that thing where she pulled her shirt off under her robe without exposing herself. She did it remarkably quickly, too. She wrapped the sleeves around Brook's neck. A red cape. "There you go."

In her white shaggy shorts, black tank and red pseudo-cape, Brooklyn did look like a superhero. A little. She lifted herself off the ground and began to fly upward.

"Sonofabitch."

I looked at Gia. "Do you think those guys at the wedding were supervillains?"

"I don't like to profile, but sure. They looked it. What the fuck is going on?"

I pointed to a bush not far from us, near a gazebo I'd never been in. Had I ever stepped foot in this courtyard of my own place? Was that even called a gazebo? I'm a terrible rich person.

She pointed at the bush with both hands.

Nothing.

I hate to see Brook disappointed. I'm the guy that adds hatch lines to her drawings at night so she thinks she's a better artist. Sometimes I have to adjust the nose. It's not a big deal except when I set my alarm to do it.

"Maybe you have different powers." I walked over to the Gazebo. There was a giant rock right in front of it. It must have weighed hundreds of pounds. It might have been a piece of art. There was a face sculpted on it. Someone signed it. I'm a terrible rich person.

"Can you lift this?"

I reconsidered that as Brook approached. The last thing I wanted was for her to be sad.

"Hey, Bitch." Gia waved from across the field. She pulled something out of her robe pocket. "There's bacon in it for you if you do."

Brook looked at me and shrugged. I won't ever forget what she did next.

She walked up to that rock and bent over. I remember thinking how well her cape moved in the wind as she lifted the rock with one hand and, in one fluid movement, sent it flying through the air until it was a tiny dot, disappearing in the Tonga blue sky.

She walked over to me just as Gia sidled up, handing her a piece of bacon. I tried to work it out in my head. I couldn't see past the main house.

"Hey. That was toward the ocean, right?"

We had dinner and drinks by the pool. The pool here is specifically designed to look natural, like an organic hot spring. It took thousands of dollars to build and is designed, essentially, to emulate a naturally occurring hot spring about a half a mile west of here. So, before you say anything, yes. I had a pool commissioned that would have happened naturally, for free, if I had had this place built a few hundred feet in that direction. Yes, I'm a terrible rich person.

"So, what do I do now?"

Gia seemed to have it figured out the quickest. "You help people. I mean, you're not a total asshole."

"True dat."

I leaned back and kicked water at her from the edge of the pool. "Hey, do you have X-ray vision?"

"How can I tell? None of you fuckers are wearing clothes."

"She got us on that one, Sunny." Gia pulled a leg up on the side of the pool so that her pussy was pointing directly at Brook like a little pink wink. I suddenly became hyper aware of where my penis was pointing.

"How do I find people to help?" This may have seemed like a dumb question, but, in reality, it was THE question.

"Ladies. I have a story."

"Ooh. storytime." Gia hopped in and they both splashed me ritually. I leaned in, sitting on the side of the pool and told them the story of spider-boy.

"Ok, people. A long time ago, Sunil was an eight year old boy who loved comic books. He especially loved Spider-man. That was his favorite superhero."

Brook raised her hand.

"You do not have to raise your hand, B."

"Are we talking about you?"

"How many Sunils do you know?"

"You're just talking about yourself in the third person. It's confusing."

"Yeah, Sun, it feels kind of artificial." Gia took a deep breath and sunk underwater .

"She'll be back. Go on."

"Ok, so I got my spider-man underwear out and put them on over my sweats. And for one full week, I snuck out every night, as soon as the sun went down, to fight crime and help people."

Gia was back up. "With great power comes great responsibility."

"Ooh, ooh, that. Exactly. Thank you. So Every single night, for a week. I'm wandering around the neighborhood looking for crime. Finally, about a week later, I saw my first crime."

"Somebody tried to get you into a van?" Gia sank back underwater.

"Yeah, pretty much. Still a crime, though."

Brooklyn scrunched up her face. "And you were wearing your underwear?"

"Moving on, I realized a really important piece of the superhero narrative. People do crime in secret."

I leaned back as if to punctuate my point. "It's really hard to find."

"Got it. Tough lesson to learn so early in life as a superhero."

"The toughest." I sighed. Brook and I sat there for a moment and considered the implications. Maybe we could connect with the facilitators somehow, help solve some of the issues that they addressed? Violent crime had gone down a huge amount since the police were dissolved and facilitators were mostly mediators and public health experts, firemen, rescue experts, etc. Someone still needed help, for sure. The night seemed quiet. Actually, it seemed overly quiet.

"Hey, B. Was it your turn to make sure Giana doesn't drown?"

"I got a lot of stuff going on in my life right now, Sun."

Suddenly Gia popped up again, slowly and looked at us.

She wiped the water out of her eyes. "Hey, guys. I don't think I need to breathe anymore."

"Go go go go," Brooklyn chanted as I watched the stopwatch hit 1,500 seconds.

'That's getting kind of old, B." How much was 1,500 seconds. For a second I regretted not setting the stopwatch to minutes. 1,500 divided by 60. I knew that 1,200 would be twenty minutes. So twenty minutes plus a bunch of minutes. I suddenly felt really stupid.

"That's twenty plus minutes. Tap her."

Gia slowly slid up again. This time she didn't need to wipe her eyes. Not gonna lie, it was a bit spooky.

Brooklyn looked right into her eyes. "Do you have brain damage?"

"Rude. Probably. Check this out."

And that's when Giana shot upward into the sky, just like Brooklyn had. She flew upward and spun in the sky, dipping down and sliding easily back into the pool.

Entirely naked.

"Wow. that was the greatest display of super public indecency I've ever seen." I was honestly impressed.

Brooklyn was chewing gum. I have no idea where she got gum. It wouldn't have been a problem, but you need to know something about B. She is very smart. Dangerously smart, in fact. She is quick, and clever, and she actually knows a couple of languages. But when she chews gum, her IQ drops by about sixty points. I have no idea why. But it's something we've all noticed.

"So, can you talk to fish?"

"Holy shit. Am I a fish girl superhero? That would be unexpected."

"How did you know you could fly?"

"I don't know. I guess it felt right. It felt like a good way to get out of the pool. Like I could do it if I tried. It's just like getting up out of a chair."

"Both of you, what else does it feel like you can do?

Brooky swam to the edge of the pool and put her hands on the rim. With a single movement, she flipped herself upside down, propped up by one hand for a full minute over the edge.

"Yah." We applauded. It was beautiful.

Giana turned to us. "Hey, guys."

She pointed toward the deck, connecting the house. The sun was starting to go down, but the house was as bright as it had been at noon. A pyre of blue fire was building right in front of the doorway. By now, the way it flickered was fairly familiar. It exploded upward and split into three pieces.

And the three supervillains from the wedding stepped out and began approaching us.

"Shit," I moved to the edge of the pool and pulled myself out. Brooklyn began to run, pulling a giant spike from the ground from the group surrounding the Gazebo. She held it like a lance and rose into the sky, coming down and stabbing the leftmost one right through the heart.

All this, so you know, with gum in her mouth.

"So, Brook is an expert assassin." Gia stood next to me and raised herself up to her full height. She started to walk toward the men. I looked down and saw the grass under her begin to die with every step. Just touching her was killing it- as it turned black and brown and dissolve. She stopped right in front of the biggest one and put out her arm.

He moved forward and his neck slid perfectly into her hand. She lifted and something bizarre happened.

His blue black skin began to darken even more, smoldering, engulfed by the black flames that raced around his body. I took a step toward her and suddenly my feet lifted off the ground. Seconds later, I was forty feet in the air watching her hold Black Aquaman above her head. Gia's eyes were black and I heard, almost as a whisper, as she said something that sounded like "It's your time, Zeriakl."

He screamed and his skin exploded outward, exposing bones covered in ruins and drawings that began to melt and blacken as he liquified, falling in pieces to the ground.

It was so much, so quickly, that I nearly forgot to notice that I was floating in the air.

I was flying, too.

It hadn't occurred to me that if both of them had gotten powers, I might, as well. I looked down and saw the third of the giant men advancing on Gia and Brook from behind. I felt in my body how I might come down fast enough to stop him. But something else welled up inside me. I opened my mouth, initially to warn the girls but then I thought better of it. I tried to catch his attention.

I took a deep breath and yelled, "Hey, asshole." I could feel the sound escaping my throat and then, suddenly, something more. My mouth shaped it and the sound grew, in a wave of transparent waves that seemed to undulate through the air. The sound that came from them was deafening and it left a massive sonic boom in its wake before the waves hit the supervillain and ripped the skin from him, compressing and shattering his bones to powder.

Both girls looked at me as I slowly came down. We stood together on the grass and watched the bloody carcasses boil away, melting into the ground.

Then Gia looked up as though she had seen something neither of us could. She stared into the empty air and listened for a second, until, suddenly, she lifted her right hand into a middle finger and addressed empty space.

"And fuck you, too."

The Hell you Are

Ok, let's back up. Right after the wedding, Zeriakl materialized in the center of a giant white room along with Kire and Nondukoma.

Kire looked up and nodded. "Well, this is looking promising."

Zeriakle shook his head. "Yeah, don't get your hopes up. This is just the clean room."

Nondukoma looked down and saw a tiny two foot tall red man with a round belly and an exposed hair-covered penis that was only centimeters away from dragging on the floor.

"Do you assholes have anything to declare?"

"I declare that you can go shove your fist up your ass, Peabody." Zeriakle grunted with frustration.

"He. Hey. Hey. Jagoff. This is my job. You want the hose, fuck your face, then, you get the hose."

Kire looked at the others, "His name is Peabody?"

Suddenly six hundred thousand gallons of hot water slammed into them with the force of a runaway train. Peabody seemed to surf above the waves of water, invading their spaces with a red and white brush.

"Get squeaky, fuckers."

Nondukoma tried to stay upright. "Zeriakle, how do you know anything about this?"

"I was trying to tell you guys. I actually have a plan. Now." He reached out and grabbed the tiny red man and with one movement, wrapped his penis around him and threw him against the wall where he made an ostentatious splat noise and popped like a zit, spraying blood everywhere. As his limp, desanguinated body fell beneath the white wave onslaught, Kire thought he could hear his voice trailing off:

"Oh, go fuck yourselves…"

The three tried to stay above the foaming white wave but soon fell into a center that began to swirl perilously like a whirlpool.

Zeriakl yelled out, "Just let go, it's ok."

Nondukoma shrugged. Now would be pretty much the worst time to stop trusting The larger Zeriakl and so he did. Letting his fingers open and free themselves from the white guardrail at the edge of the room and his body sink into the powerful eddy.

A minute or so later, they found themselves on their backs in the middle of a massive red space, filled with speculative eyes on the far end drenched in darkness. In front of them was a massive red throne with a twenty foot tall Demonic figure. He was red all over with black veins throughout and a simian like face. Two massive leathery red wings spread behind him, twitching occasionally, as if by their own will. He leaned over the side of the throne and lifted a large red towel from beside him, throwing it at Zeriakl. He stared at him and then, with a snarl, implored:

"You could wipe up a bit."

Zeriakl began the task of drying himself, making sure to dry his boots and pants. He didn't want to trudge water everywhere.

"We're trying. That always just seems excessive."

The Demon sat up straight. "You're coming from Earth. Do you have any idea the kind of viruses and shit they have on earth? It's like licking a toilet.

Do you want to lick a toilet?"

Nondukoma looked up and began drying himself as well. "No, sir."

Zeriakl stared daggers at him. He mouthed "I got this," to the two others. They nodded.

Now, we've been dancing around this for a bit, but it's starting to get awkward in the prose itself. So let's be clear about who these three are. Up until earlier that day, they were all members of the Angelic host - Angels in good standing. Until they decided to be fallen. And there is a word for that, too. Something that they would have to get used to being called.

"Demons, come on over. Take a look. This is how NOT to travel back and forth from earth. Do you know they have something on earth called the Hamster flu that actually evolved from snakes eating dying hamsters and then getting eaten by humans." The Red demon shook his head.

"I don't think that one's true," Kire said, drying himself off.

"Whatever. Stay on the carpet until you're dry."

"Lucifer, my lord, Lightbringer, Samael, Lord of Darkness, We meet you well." Zeriakl read this off a small piece of rumpled brown paper he had stored in his boot. He looked around at all the demons who had assembled all around them now. Truth to tell he had no idea where this was going to go.

"Bla bla, it's all good. Look, you're not coughing. It's all good. We're safe. Just got to stay alert, you know. Good to see you guys. I'm Satan. Lucy.

"I'm Nondukoma. I was the Uriel, responsible for enlightenment."

The ring of Demons around him spoke in Unison, "Hello, Uriel."

"Hey. Hey, cut it out. If we do that for everyone we'll be here all fucking day." Satan turned apologetically to Nondukoma, "If we do that, we'll just... you know... drag it out."

"Hi, I'm Kire."

Satan raised his fist as if to do a long distance fist bump. It was incredibly unsatisfying. "And the big guy is Zeraikl. Inspiration. Nice. "

"Thanks for. Well, thank you for not, you know, destroying us."

Satan stepped back over to his throne. "Destroying? Guys. You rebelled. You're fallen. You're one of us now. We got your back. I mean, it was not a very, you know, powerful rebellion, but all the same…"

"We turned our back on the almighty."

"Did you, though? Really. You made a toast. You didn't… But, you know what, it's all good. Times are different. You're alive, it's all good."

"I thought you'd be happier." Zeriakl advanced toward the throne.

"Well. I thought we talked about what we needed to do."

"We killed the Postate. The field should be clear for you."

"Do me a favor, Kleiger, come here." Stan looked around in the crowd. A large, twelve foot tall orange skeleton covered in black and gray fur stepped up and took two steps toward the throne.

"Ah, good, Kleiger, look, punch that guy in the tongue."

"Shit, What did I do?" Zeriakl looked scared as the horrific demon approached.

"Just put your fist right in the mouth, there. Get it in."

"Ok, I'm sorry, I am. What's wrong?"

"Fuck. Kleiger, stand down." Satan looked at Zeriakl. "Big baby. No, you didn't kill the postate. She survived. And she has Hierarchy now."

Nondukoma looked up. 'Wait, what? We saw her die."

"Well, she made it and she now has Heavenly host to protect her.

"Wait. she anointed Host. What the fuck. How did she do that already?" Zeriakl was confused.

Satan shook his head, "You can't feel it? People, am I imagining shit?"

There were murmurs in the room, then a resounding "NO."

Kire looked penitent. "Tell us what to do and we'll do it."

Satan looked up. "Tell you what to do? I don't think you understand how this works." He looked around the room and then said, mockingly, "Ohh, I'm a big Pussy, Satan made me do it. Wah."

Getting up, he brushed himself off.

"And can I get one of those Sticky brush things for the outfit, please. Anyone?"

Nondukoma looked sincere, "Whatever we need to do, right?"

"Tell you what to do. Ha. What do YOU guys think?"

The demons in a circle around them began to scream and throw things at them. They swirled around and built into a blue fire. It covered the ground beneath them, dragging them in and dropping them, as though they had fallen through a trap door. Seconds later, the air righted itself and there was no sign of the portal.

Satan yelled out, "Ok, ok." He tossed a towel to the nearest demon. "Here. Clean that up.

"Fucking unbelievable."

The three demons reappeared in the center of the ballroom. A few feet away, hotel employees were in the center of the room cleaning blood from the floor. Zeriakl noticed, for the first time, the odd patterns in the rug.

"Hey, guys." he pointed downward and started walking in a circle. "Do these look like sacred writings to you?"

Nondukoma cocked his head. "I didn't notice those last night."

"Hey, m'man." Kire called out to one of the guys cleaning the carpet. He was a shorter man, seemingly Mexican, in a blue and gray maintenance uniform. His nametag sad "Ramone."

Ramone looked up and saw the demons there. He shook his head a little. A student of human nature and keen observer of nuances in gestures might have concluded that he was frustrated by the various intrusions that prevented him from doing his job quickly and quietly, regardless of how truly interesting those intrusions were.

Before falling, Kire was, in fact, the Raguel, which made him the angel of justice. His job was to see inside men, to determine what was just, to ensure justice. And after 400,000 years, those instincts were still very much alive.

Kire's eyes turned black as he did the math in his head. Ramone likely was paid about twenty five dollars an hour. In his head, he probably broke work down into groupings of an hour or so, since most maintenance tasks required at least a little focus and shifting of perspective. Four hours would be a fine unit of work for him to consider. One hundred dollars. If he were to receive ten times that for a short interval that wouldn't prevent him from keeping to his schedule, he would likely consider that just.

"I can give you a thousand dollars if you answer a couple of questions for a few minutes." Kire pulled the money out from the front of his pants and showed him.

Ramone bounced up with surprising grace and wiped his hands on the towel he was using.

"Got it, boss." He took the money and put it in his pocket.

"What do you guys need to know?"

"What happened here?" Nondukoma figured it would help to get a baseline.

"Oh, so last night they had this big Richie Rich wedding here. One bottle of the wine would have put my kids through school. Anywho, some big guys ripped someone's arm off and nearly killed Emma."

Zeriakl perked up. "Wait, you know her name? The Woman?"

"Yeah, boss. Emma Jackson. Funny story, she actually works here as a maid and then somebody hired her to come to the wedding and sing at the end. She's a singer. Beautiful voice."

"So she was here, as a guest?" Zeriakl was putting some pieces together.

"Yep. These guys tried to strangle her. Some people at the wedding stopped them and then helped get her to the hospital. But she's fine."

Kire asked, "So, when is she back to work here?"

Ramone looked particularly satisfied at this, "That's just it. She quit right BEFORE the wedding so she wasn't here as an employee. So that means she's owed a big settlement from the hotel. It'll be sweet."

"Before the wedding? Are you sure?"

"Yep. The email went out before the wedding."

"Do you know what hospital they took her to?"

"Nah, man. We've just been here trying to clean stuff up and make this all presentable. There's another event here tonight. Like a dental thing. You good?"

Zeriakl sighed, "Yes, we're good. Oh, wait, one last thing, Ramone?

"Yeah, boss."

"How long has this carpet been like this?"

"Oh, the pattern? I've been here twenty years and it's always been like this. Wait. Maybe not. Hm. No, that's new."

Zeriakl ordered a chai from the busty heavily pierced and tattooed cafe waitress as he tried to adjust himself in a booth that was many times too small for him. Nondukoma had acquired a phone and had placed it on the table's receptive surface. Thin,reddish orange lines of coherent light spread out from the device, creating the visual perception of a keyboard on the table, along with a screen. Kire moved the screen with his fingers so that it would be easier for them all to see while he blew on his black coffee.

"It's always a little too hot."

"How do you guys know how to do all this?"

Nondukoma looked up at him, "We spend a lot more time here than you. Besides, I was, essentially, the archangel of wisdom." He said that sadly.

"I know this is hard. I'm trying to save our lives. Notice who is gone and who is still here."

Kire looked down. Despite being the smallest of the three, he was a huge man. All of this, the events of the last few days, though, had gotten him to feel very small, for sure.

"I hate to say it, but I'm going to miss him."

"Whom are you missing?"

"You know. Aya. I miss him already."

"This was his decision." Zeriakl seemed angry. "And he didn't include any of us in it.

"I know, I know. I just. You know."

So, reader. I am keenly aware that you don't know. So, while the three demons order a light meal to go with their coffee and experiment with what actual food tastes like, here goes.

About 400,354 years ago, There were a number of races of man walking around the planet. This was about 100,000 years before we'd see a Homo Sapiens, though. But still, many kinds of man, including Heanderthals and Homo Rhodesiensis, an offshoot of Homo Heidelbergensis living in Africa, often known as Rhodesian man.

Well, that was what people called them when they were discovered by Arthur Smith Woodward in 1921 based on a broken piece of bone called the Kabwe skull. He named the species to honor a truly shitty man named Cecil Rhodes, a diamond magnate who was a scurrilous racist. After that was discovered, the species was renamed Homo Bodoensis. But, during their lifetimes, way back when, they referred to themselves as "Go Kor" or "the thick ones." This was mostly due to the fact that, of all the species of man that were around at the time, they had the thickest faces, widest necks, etc.

They were thick.

And thousands of them lived across the area we know of as Zambia today. And one of them was a twenty two year old man named Aya. He was a hunter and an inventor. His claim to fame, amongst his friends, was discovering that rubbing softer stones against harder ones could render them sharper so that they would stab or cut better.

If you are a 400,000 year old hunter, I cannot overestimate what a beautiful invention this was. For the people in his tribe, it literally changed everything. His tribe eventually became known far and wide as "Go ke Maka" or "The ones who cut."

If that sounds super badass to you, imagine how badass it was back then. Do you want to wage war against "the ones who cut?"

Didn't think so.

So, it goes without saying that Aya was well liked amongst his people. He was handsome, he was taller than most, although it seemed like much of that was in his legs. He was dark and mysterious looking and the women flocked to him like Prehistoric boars on a ripe berry bush. He ended up marrying a couple of wonderful people and settling down into a pretty comfortable routine.

For his people, definitely.

Aya started to do what he had always wanted to do. Have as many kids as he could. Not long before that, his people had discovered the connection between sex and having children. Again, big discovery, it led to some really fun moments. Aya was a fan of children and, it turns out, a big fan of making them.

So as Aya entered his thirties, we see a very content and happy young H. Bodoensis with a tribe who loved him, a big polycule of a family he loved, all the real life porn he could ever want, and a brood of kids on the way.

Not long after, He figure-eight rope tied a long straight stick to one of his famous cutting stones and invented the spear. This sophomore effort was maybe even more popular than his first one, and soon every person of means in the entire area had a spear. His now seven year old oldest son Goro became the first child to effectively throw a spear, sending a sharp stone right through the eye socket and into the brain of a large boar.

Imagine being seven years old and doing something like that- something that will make you peak marriage material for the rest of your life. That kid could have just sat back and gotten fat and would still have been the most eligible bachelor in human history, He had a line of spears named after him. He was the Michael Jordan of the Middle Pleistocene Era.

Life was good for Aya. He was all the things he wanted to be. A lover, an inventor, a success, a friend…

But mostly, he was a father.

When he woke up, he played with his kids. He explored with his kids. He snuck up on his wives and husbands and playfully stole the kids away when they weren't looking to play airplane through the forest. He raced his kids, fed his kids, taught his kids.

And he loved his kids. All day long. Aya's home, the biggest amongst all his people, was always full of the holiest sound in the world, the sound of children laughing. The neighborhood children came to play, too.

No one resented him or denied him the biggest parts of the kill. He never asked for it. But he Was Aya, and the tribe loved him. He felt blessed by Kuthau, the god of his people - the god of everything.

As his kids got older, they survived the small challenges that were commonplace in the area. But one day, his youngest, Kawa, took ill. Her eyes were puffy and her skin lost its color and hung off her face. When she died, Aya felt as though he had been stabbed through the heart with one of his own spears.

Soon, it became clear that this sickness wasn't done taking lives. It made its way through Aya's seven children, wreaking havoc, killing indiscriminately, until only Goro, his oldest, was left.

And less than two weeks from Goro's tenth birthday, he died as well.

The entire tribe was inconsolate. But Aya, himself, was out of his mind. He went to the K'lau - the highest spot in the village - a small mountain top. He pulled off all his clothes and ranted, screaming, yelling, his head up to the sky. Aya wasn't mad at anyone in the village.

Aya was mad at God. He addressed Kuthau by name. He screamed until his voice was gone. And Kuthau heard him.

Kuthau descended and explained to him that he sympathized. Aya was angry and barely heard him when he explained that, according to the rules, if someone truly believed that he could be a better god and made their case well, God had no choice but to consider it.

To consider stepping down and giving them the power.

And Aya made his case. Kuthau explained to him that while he couldn't bring his own children back as they were, he could make the world what he wanted from here on.

And Aya took the job.

Some people called him Yahweh, which was an honest mistake.

Some people called him Allah. Which was also understandable.

Some people called him Abba, which was a bit more of a stretch

He was called Elohim, which is like the last go round in a game of telephone. But you can see it.

And when Emma Jackson wrote her song, telling him she could do a better job, she just called him God.

Again With The Wedding

Walking down the hallway, Emma considered the results of her meeting with God, thinking about the end of her conversation in much the same way that many people consider their prayers after they have been said.

I'll think about it.

Was she honestly considering taking the job of God?

Well, there were pros and cons, honestly. Especially since it wasn't real.

Emma stopped off at the cart she had left down the hall. She stopped and pulled off her maid uniform over her head. Leaning against the cart she removed the comfortable flats that she wore every day to work and tossed them into the trash bag.

A young couple made their way down the corridor and slowed, seeing her standing there in her pale bra and unmatched underwear.

"What are you looking at? That's right. Move on."

She'd been a maid at this hotel for over ten years. She'd behaved perfectly that entire time. Not that it mattered. When she needed time off to spend with her son, dying of Leukemia in a nearby cancer ward, she was told no.

Just no.

Sending that resignation email was satisfying. But it was made more so by her decision to kill herself in that unmade room. Death would be relaxing, she had thought, but the attention drawn to the hotel would shut it down for days, at least. They would complain.

And the facilitators would say no.

And that felt a little good.

The pros of being God? Well no more nine to five job. She pushed the uniform down deeper into the trash bag. She should have burned it, she thought. But that just seemed like more work at this time.

She knocked over the cart. They were made not to fall over. It actually took some effort to do it. But, finally, she managed to lay it down in the middle of the corridor.

That was a little satisfying. You take your victories where you can.

She picked up the universal keycard.

Time to go shopping.

It took three rooms to find someone who was about the same size. Emma had to admit she was little. And right now maybe a little curvier than she really wanted. Maybe being homeless would give her a chance for some cardio.

Or she could always just take the job. The cons of the imaginary job?

Pretty much everything. It's the biggest job in the universe, isn't it? That usually comes with overtime. It comes with headaches.

It comes with pain.

She saw the pain in God's eyes. And while he watched her die, she watched him.

She watched his eyes.

It's hard to believe that his eyes were that cruel when he was a human.

Being god would mean watching people die every day. Watching people descend into the worst pain imaginable. Being God would be like standing watch over a billion cancer wards, watching a billion children die slowly and doing nothing because surely there were rules, ways of behaving, things that an all powerful being couldn't do to ease the pain of a small child and make them think that the world wasn't just full of pain.

God had given her until midnight to decide. That seemed like a ridiculously short amount of time to decide the fate of the entire universe.

But that was life, right? Never enough of anything, really. She looked through the closet of room 565. She liked this woman's style, honestly. And she had arranged her dresses according to color, making the inside of that closet look vaguely like a fancy neighborhood thrift store.

She pulled a green dress out from the rest, nestled between a black one and a brighter green one. It was classy and pretty. And she spotted some matching size eight shoes on the way in.

The one thing she did feel good about was this. Last week, a pretty Muslim woman came up to her after her open mic and asked if she would come sing at her wedding. One song, open mic. Emma was honored and said yes, but really didn't think she'd be able to be there.

But now she could.

She looked at herself in the full length mirror. The collar of the dress went up high enough to cover the marks in her neck. That was helpful. That meant she wouldn't be explaining to strangers all night why it looked like she'd gone on a date with the Boston Strangler. The few marks that showed could be covered in makeup. She grabbed some makeup from the woman's makeup bag on the desk and made her way to an empty room.

There was an unbooked room just three doors down, room 559.

Emma sat down to do her makeup. Every day when you do your makeup, it's like a commitment to something. To inventing yourself. To preparing yourself. To protecting yourself. She thought about how doing your makeup could feel like going to war.

Tonight she would go and wind down her life.

She would sit at a table and watch some people begin their lives together. She would have a drink or two and then sing a song for the last time, in front of people. That was always her favorite thing in the world. She lived for that moment right before the first note. When people were ready, open, listening. That was the moment anything could happen.

She would make her peace with all of it. And might even dance a little.

And then she would find a quiet place and say no, thank you to God. She would thank him and ask him to move on to the next candidate. And she would find a way to go to sleep for the last time.

Emma checked out her dress and makeup from all angles. Stepping out of the room, she threw the universal keycard down the hallway. It was unweighted so it didn't go very far. Someone had picked up the cart she had left tipped over and cleaned up the fallen rack of towels.

Why was it so hard to leave behind some mayhem?

She sighed and walked toward the elevators.

She could already hear the life infecting the entire hotel from the wedding below. When the doors opened on three it was an explosion of sound, of light, of joy.

Emma wasn't often on the first three floors, reserved for big events. And she had never been on the third floor, the one that contained the largest banquet hall in the city. This was generally where politicians and celebrities were wed, amidst thousands of cheering fans. This was a whole different world than the one that Emma was used to.

Up against the interior wall there were about eight tables full of little figures. She looked down and couldn't believe how pretty they were.

The wedding planners had made these little figurines to reflect each of the thousands of wedding guests. She ran her finger along the table and saw hers. Sitting on a card that said "Emma Jackson" was a beautiful figurine of a frog princess with a microphone, singing.

Emma smiled and realized that they were all frogs. Every figurine was a frog. She saw a frog doctor, a frog dancer, and various Frogs doing random things. For a second her eyes were drawn to a dashing frog holding up a phone camera and posing with his two female frog friends. One of them was holding up her shirt and flashing the camera. The little scene made her laugh out loud.

And the card under the tiny sculpture read "Sunil Aram and friends."

Emma nodded. This looked like a party she could get behind.

There was something liberating about knowing how her night would end. Emma realized that she could just let go. In a way, she had lived her life like someone who was afraid she'd left the gas on at home. She'd gone through everyday waiting for the other shoe to drop - waiting for it to end somehow and be her fault.

Tonight would be different.

She picked up her frog and read the card. It was sweet and ended with a table number.

You know you're at a bg wedding when your table number is three figures. Emma moved toward the table, navigating the maze of tables and carts that arrayed themselves around the room.

"Em!" a thin blonde girl in a bartender's uniform came up from behind her.

Emma was startled then hugged her. "Betina," You're working this?

"I am. Thanks to you."

Emma adjusted her collar, "Oh, girl, I had nothing to do with it."

Betina grabbed her by the arm, "Yeah you did. Um…" She quoted Emma, "while her work, attention to detail, and learning curves are impressive, Betina may be more useful in a capacity where her bright and sunny demeanor can create positive experiences for the clientele daily."

"I think I was just saying you were too fucking happy to be a maid."

"I think they got that. Happy enough to be a bartender."

"Are you liking it?" Emma stepped toward the bar with her.

"Are you kidding? Do you know what the tips are like here as a bartender? The job is great, but I would literally cut my eyelids off with an exacto blade every night for these tips."

Betina slid behind the bar. "What do you want, girl? I'd buy you a drink but this is an open bar so.."

Emma looked behind her. "I can't decide."

Betina looked at the pretty Latina woman sitting next to Emma, "Excuse me, pretty lady. If I could make you anything in the world, which, let's face it, I can, what would you be drinking exactly one minute from now?"

"I am so about that question. Hm. A lemon drop?" the woman answered.

"Good answer. Coming up."

"Can I get two? I have a gay friend."

Betina winked at her and looked up at Emma, "Three?"

Emma thought for a sec. "I'm kind of stepping away from those. How about a Watermelon Redbull Vodka with a lime."

The woman looked over. "Ok, now that actually sounds better. Two of those?"

Betina stepped back. "Got it."

"I quit today." It felt good to Emma to say it out loud. It made it real. She held up her drink and nodded to the Latin woman going back to her table.

"Are you going to sing for a living?" Betina looked excited.

"Well, I'm singing tonight."

"Oh my god. I haven't seen you sing in months. That makes me so happy. I'm gonna scream so loud. " Betina made a motion to yell silently.

"I forgot how much I missed you, girl." Emma took a sip of her drink. Did she like it better than the drink made by God? Maybe.

"Do you believe in God?"

Betina looked up. "Hm. Good question. I think I do not. I think the world can be so cruel and people just lean into it, you know. If God were real would he let that happen?"

"I guess I think the same."

"I'll go to church with my grandpa every once in a while. I mean, I believe in HIM."

"Is he cool?"

"You would love my grandpa. Love Love Love. He loves the old singers, too. Like Doja Cat and SZA."

"Those were good times for music."

"Yeah. I get it. I mean I like modern stuff, too, like the Rejection and XOC, but they were something back then."

"Yep."

"But my grandpa believes. And I think he thinks it makes him a better person."

"To believe that there is a god out there?"

"To even think about it." Betina came around to the front of the bar and sat next to her with her own drink.

"You're on break?"

"For another fifteen minutes. I was just walking around."

They walked back to Emma's table, passing a thin but tall young server. Betina grabbed the plate from his hand.

"Emad, this is Emma, she used to work here until today. Emma, this is Emad, he's giving us this whole plate of appetizers."

"I am. Take them and go in peace. I'll get another plate."

"Thank you Emad," Emma yelled after him. "What a nice boy."

"I steal from him all the time. I might follow him home one day and steal."

"Get your fun where you can."

"Exactly." She looked so happy. And the plate full of tiny food was a solid idea right now. "This is your table?"

"That's what the frogs say."

"I like it. You've got a view of everything. The people getting married here have more money than you can imagine."

"I wonder what that's like?"

"I think it's all about how you use it, right?"

"Yes, but is there a fair and just way to even HAVE that much money? You could have been working your job with the great tips since Dinosaurs were here, on this planet, and you still wouldn't have what the richest people do. And they spend it on this."

The lights in the room dropped a bit as the ceiling of the room lit up. Billions of light points turned it into a screen and the announcer announced The loving couple. It was a really beautiful display.

But it must have cost a fortune.

Betina raised her drink to the people on the screen and Emma joined her.

"To the giant happy couple people."

"Where can they even honeymoon, they're so big?"

"At some point, it's basically a disability."

Just then, the center of the room came alive with a giant hologram of the Imam consecrating the ceremony.

"Wow."

"Yeah, he big, too." Emma drank again.

"Are we drunk?"

"Not yet. Isn't your break over?"

"Yeah, they'll fill in for me until I get back. Everyone wants the tips, you know. In the middle of all these giant people, I just wanted to spend a little time with my tiny little friend."

"That's sweet."

"Tiny Emma. Little bitty Em."

"Ok, I'm not that little. Have a meatball."

She shoved a meatball into Betina's mouth. Bartenders need to have a little more leg if they wanted to drink like that. "You should eat some, girl."

"It's loud in here."

"Well, it looks like everyone in the zip code is here, so."

"No doubt."

Across from her, at the table, a man sat down in a purple jacket. Emma lifted her drink and nodded at him. He looked kind. Like most people here, he was middle eastern. He had an easy smile, and he flashed it at her.

She looked back at Betina.

If this was her last day it was good to spend it with friends and nice people. It was good to spend it doing things she loved. It was good to be alive for a while.

She wasn't sure if she could have survived it right away when Kai died without Betina. She was good to her. She tried to make her laugh and then, when that didn't happen she just let her be sad. She quietly worked alongside her some days, eating lunch with her.

It's a heroic act sometimes for an essentially happy person to stand by and exist next to someone who is sad, crushed, dying inside. To not run for their own life. To not skitter off to be with their happy friends. And to not force change that had to happen in its own gradual way.

Betina was a hero. She earned her stars being quiet and present on days where she could have been in other rooms, lighting them up with happy people. Secretly, Emma dedicated this drink to her.

She lifted her glass. Over the top of it she saw a giant man with near blue-black skin and dreads moving toward her. Right behind him were two others.

What were they up to?

Then, suddenly, the Larger of the men picked up the table next to them and threw it, causing a mass exodus from the area. Betina still looked a little drunk. Emma stood up, pushing her under the table. The man in the purple jacket got up, too, quickly moving around the table to confront the men who now seemed to be bearing down on Emma quite purposefully.

One of the men reached over and, without fanfare, lifted up the man and ripped his arm clean off.

The room erupted into screams.

Emma looked down. Betina was huddled under the table, lost. She shushed her and confronted the men. The two slightly smaller ones flanked the table and began fighting off all the people who were determined to help. Emma realized, though, quickly, that this was about her. The facial features of these men seemed to reflect much of what she had seen in God's face. It wasn't hard to imagine that these events might be connected. The largest man felt familiar.

He reached down and grabbed her by the neck. White hot knives shot through Emma's body, reminding her of the hour she had spent with her neck breaking and splitting over and over again up in that room. The man's hand dug into it much like the noose had. She looked up into his face and realized that she did recognize him. But it wasn't the human side of her, the part that was Emma Jackson, that did. It wasn't the recognition of one person for another person.

It was something different.

She tried to speak but nothing came out. She reached up to put her hands up, to try and pry his thick, rough hand from her neck, but he may as well have been a metal clamp, a machine, determined to break her.

He crushed her windpipe and a part of her realized that she would never speak as a human being ever again. That much was true. But at this point, there was only one decision she had left that she could make.

As her vision narrowed, she considered her earlier decision to die and the peace it had brought her. She could choose that peace right now and let herself go.

Her brain reminded her ominously that the opposite of peace was usually war. But maybe not this time.

As the dark closed in, she thought one word.

"yes"

Veridian Skies

Adam covered the distance from the bank to the skate park in seconds, dropping from the freeway level to the pedestrian level by way of a forty five foot tall light pole. He slid down it, making a mental note that this part had actually taken LESS time than they had practiced. He spun around and dashed through the morass of skaters that they had anticipated would make the local facilitators think twice before trying to shoot. If he could reach the tunnels within the next minute, they would all be gone.

In Manhattan, it used to be that only fifteen or twenty percent of bank robberies were ever solved. The dissolution of the police left funding for the kind of facilitation that managed bank robberies as thought experiments. And suddenly that number almost tripled. For robberies that didn't involve weapons, there was a slightly lower solve rate. But this one had. And someone had gotten hurt, which is something that Adam would definitely hold the responsible party accountable for.

For him, this was meant to be fun. He grew up on a Parkour Farm, where he and his friends were raised to treat urban areas as an obstacle course they could take in and triumph over. It wasn't in his heart to hurt people and, as far as he was concerned, Bryan, with the quick trigger finger and easily angered machismo that made him shoot that poor man in the chest, was off the team.

For good.

He saw the tunnel ahead of him. It was unobstructed and clear.

Until suddenly it wasn't

The black center began to sprout and vines, leaves, bushes emerged, choking the tunnel and filling it with life. Adam tried to evaluate the situation without stopping. He dove to the left and kept running. What just happened was impossible. It was like nothing he'd ever seen.

And then it happened again. The path in front of him grew thick and full, vines shot out of the ground and grabbed his legs. He looked down. And ran directly into a tree that he could have sworn was not there a second ago.

Vines wrapped around him. He shifted, trying to face outward at least, before they fully tightened. His chest felt compressed and he dropped the bag of money on the ground. Breathing heavily he stopped.

He wasn't going anywhere.

A woman dropped from the sky in front of him. She wore a mask that covered the upper part of her face and a thin fashionable costume with black leggings and a blue and green color theme. Stepping closer, she picked up the bag of money.

"The facilitators will be here soon, but I don't want this to get lost."

"Fuck. Who are you?"

"Do you really care? You and your friends just left a guy to die." She made a motion to fly off.

"Wait, I do care. I'm sorry. Is he ok?" Adam had been worried since he ran from the bank.

The woman turned back to him. "Will you confess? If I tell you?"

"Yes, I will. For real. Just tell me how he is. Is he ok?"

"Yes. I healed him. It's one of the things I can do. Then I took off after you. He's with his family already."

Adam slumped. "Oh, thank god. I didn't want anyone to get hurt. Thank you."

He seemed sincere. "What's your friend's name who shot him?"

Adam looked at her. Her eyes made him feel better. He felt like a whole person again, someone who could do the right thing. "His name is Bryan. Bryan Reagan. I think he was just spooked and it made him angry. He didn't want to hurt anyone."

"Ok. And you'll tell them that when they come get you?"

"I will."

"You made me chase you through an area filled with kids. That was bullshit, you know."

"I do. I'm sorry. Who are you?"

"I'm a superhero." Adam felt as though the top were removed from a can he'd lived in his whole life. Superheroes were real? He remembered being younger, wanting to be one. Wanting to do the right thing. What happened?

"What's your name?"

"Fuck me, you're Veridian?"

"Shh. Not so loud." Syndra pulled Max into an empty room. They both wore grey scrubs and badges marking them as RNs but that's where the resemblance ended. Syndra was a petite Half Chinese woman of twenty four with long brown hair, accented with golden streaks. She was pretty with wide eyes but was often accused of being overly stern looking. She made a point to practice looking cheerful in the mirror at night.

Max was tall and wide. His friends always joked he had the heart of a dancer and the body of a linebacker.

He was silly and fun and harmless but his frequent walks across the city in headphones left him with leg muscles that often told a different story.

"You're a superhero." Max was clearly overwhelmed as he tried to whisper.

"For like three days."

"Still, that's amazing. You're saving people."

"What do you think we do here?"

"That's different."

"It's really not."

"What can you do?"

Syndra looked around. It was exciting to finally tell someone. "Max, it's so cool. I can make plants grow. I can fly. I can heal people."

"Shut up. Wait. Eugenia in 200?"

"Yes, that was me. You can't tell anyone."

"Oh my god. That's crazy. She was on death's door. Have you been..."

"Bits here and there. I don't want to draw too much attention. You can help me."

"What do you need?"

"I think I can help Mr. O'donnel, but I may need you to fake a test result."

"Yes."

"Wait, you don't have to think about it?"

"Fuck that. Do I have to think about it? I'll fake every document in this building if we can stop someone from dying of cancer."

"Are you sure?"

"Woman, This is a superhero costume, too. When I put these scrubs on, I will do anything I need to."

"You're the best."

The clatter of a cart overturning suddenly drew Max's attention. "Shit. What now?"

He stepped out of the room and instantly pulled back in, grabbing Syndra's arm. "Girl, do you have the costume?

She lifted her scrubs a bit and flashed the costume underneath. "Why?"

"This looks like a job for you."

Max grabbed a chair and opened the door, charging into the corridor. Syndra quickly pulled off her scrubs and lifted the mask up over her face. She took a deep breath and closed her eyes. She could feel the life energies in the corridor as they moved around. Three large men stood there towering over the staff. The security guards were already incapacitated, but alive, lying on the floor.

The men approached Max, who was brandishing a chair. Syndra took note of the locations and flew

She punched directly through the wall and into the three men, sending them scattering down the hallway like bowling pins. She turned to look at max who smiled.

"Look, everyone. It's Veridian. Where could she have come from?"

Ok. That was laying it on a bit thick, Syndra thought. But it was fun to have an ally.

The Biggest of the men got up.

"Ok, people, no one's looking for a fight. Just tell me where Emma Jackson is. I need to have a... Conference with her.

Syndra took a step. She was overwhelmed with ideas on how to handle the situation. She'd never felt that way before.

Suddenly, she was so inspired to create a brilliant solution to this problem.

Maybe she'd write a book about it later.

A chair went sailing across the hallway and hit the large man in the face. It seemed to interrupt his concentration for a moment.

"Fuck, these people are annoying. You two, find the woman."

Syndra reached out and felt the flowers sitting in the cart in the hallway. She took a deep breath and the flowers expanded, growing to fill every space, trapping the two other men. The one in front advanced. The nurses advanced, too. Syndra looked behind her and saw that the nurses weren't going anywhere.

A shorter woman in her fifties walked up to the man in a matter-of-fact way and handed him a document. It was Jill, the head floor nurse.

The large blue-black man looked at the document. "What is this?"

"These are discharge papers. Ms. Jackson was discharged five days ago and she left on her own, against doctor's advice. She hasn't checked in, although we couldn't tell you if she did. In fact, showing you this paper is violating HIPAA seven different ways. But that's how much I want you to leave my floor and let me attend to those men."

Syndra had already gotten the security guards on their feet. Samuel had a broken leg but that was easily healed. She motioned to him to walk it off.

Zeriakl rolled his eyes.

"Son of a bitch."

And the three of them disappeared in an inferno of blue flame.

The hallway was silent for a moment.

Max looked over at Syndra in costume. He started chanting.

"Veridian, Veridian, Veridian."

All the nurses began chanting. Syndra looked out and saw the people she respected most in the world chanting her name.

It was amazing.

Then, she held up her hand. Everyone stopped. Syndra smiled and chanted,

"Jill, Jill, Jill, Jill"

And the room erupted into chants and cheers,

"Jill, Jill, Jill, Jill"

Jill shook her head and looked out, she mouthed under her breath, "idiots"

And then she walked back to the Nurses' station.

The three demons reappeared in a hallway.

Zerakle sighed. "Can you guys give me a tiny bit of space?"

"It's just a bit cramped here."

"I know, but you've basically been up my ass for the whole last week."

Kire looked around, "It smells like dog in here."

Zeriakle knocked on the unassuming door. He heard some shuffling from the other side of the door. Just as he was about to knock again, the door opened.

It was Ramone. Holding his toothbrush up, casually brushing his teeth. He was still in his work pants, but he had traded the shirt for a pajama top covered in Ducks. He didn't appear surprised.

"Hey."

"We just had one more question?"

Kire leaned around and looked at him, "Do you need more money?"

Ramone continued to brush his teeth, shaking his head quickly as if to say, "it's all good."

"We won't keep you but we can't seem to locate Miss Jackson. We've been looking through hospitals for a few days"

Ramone shrugged. He didn't know where she was, either.

Nondukoma leaned in. "Let me ask you. Did anything ELSE weird happen that night?"

Ramone thought, letting his eyes drift upward. He held up a finger and disappeared for a minute, finally returning with a glass of water. He took a swig, gargled for a second, then spit it back out in the cup.

"Only little things. Some guy was running around the wedding without a shirt on. That was weird. Oh, and the teleporters on the second to last top floor got used. First time in a month.

"Teleporters?" This was news to Zeriakl

"Yeah, the rich people use them sometimes. It costs like 30 grand per person per trip."

"Can you tell where people teleported to?" Kire thought this was kind of fascinating.

"Kind of. The machine doesn't tell you, but the advertisements on it are always for the last place people teleported to.

"That's weird." Nondukoma tried to wrap his head around it.

Zeriakl sighed. "That's capitalism."

"Veridian stood on the roof of the hospital with her loyal sidekick, Max, looking out on the city that she loved and protected."

"You are so much more into this than even I am." Syndra laughed.

Max giggled, "Yes, I am. This is crazy, I'm here with a real live superhero."

"Ok, you moved Ms. Ramirez into the room by the cathedral?"

"I did that like three hours ago."

"Ok, so when her heart problems go away, they're just going to say it's from prayer, right?"

"I got the whole family praying overtime. I brought them rosaries. I got this." Max marked each off on a little checklist.

"And you erased Milton's records from General?"

"I did. That's how you handle a pre-existing condition. Ha."

"Excellent. His liver's always been in fine shape."

"That's what the paperwork says. And paperwork is never wrong."

"I really appreciate you helping me like this."

"Are you kidding? This is the most fun I've ever had. I'm breaking rules, fucking up paperwork, and healing people all at the same time. Those are literally my three favorite things. And I can do it while drinking overpriced Lattes, which is number four."

Syndra closed her eyes and tried again.

"Can you feel where she is?

"No. Not yet. It's getting stronger. Like I can feel she's here in the city."

"What do you think they wanted with Emma Jackson?"

"I don't know. But they didn't look like people who liked the word 'no'. I'm sure they're still looking to find her."

"Well, not if you find her first."

"I hope so. I'm so new at this."

"Ok, so can you look in me? Like that? I mean, how's my health?"

"Max, you're probably the healthiest thing in Manhattan. Look at you."

"No lie, I feel good."

"I can't help but think that someone like you should have been the superhero. I mean, you even LOOK like a superhero."

"Girl, all the black superheroes have lightning powers. Besides, do they have gay heroes?"

"They sure do. And I think I'm bi."

"Really? How did I never know that?"

"The same reason I barely do. I never date anyone. I have resting bitch face."

"You have a beautiful face. Shut up. Somewhere out there is a beautiful- or handsome superhero for you to team up with."

Syndra laughed. "A team up, huh?"

Max's voice lowered. "A naked team up." He handed her the coffee and Syndra grabbed it, taking a sip.

Number four was pretty good, too.

The room was white and antiseptic.

Nondukoma looked around, "Hey guys, what does THIS remind you of?"

Kire nodded, "yes, eerie. A lot of white."

"Do you guys see it anywhere?"

"What does a teleporter even look like?" Nondukoma tried to imagine, but he kept seeing HG Wells type period images in his head. This bright white space felt too- Medicinal.

Zeriakl almost bumped into it. It was sleek and plastic looking.

"A white thing in a white room."

"Do you see any advertisements?" Kire was looking all over.

"I do not."

"It all seems so quiet." Zeriakl stepped onto the platform and the wall behind him lit up.

"Make Tonga your next vacation home. The Polynesian Islands have everything, everything but you."

He stepped off and the wall went dead.

Nondukoma looked over, "Where was that?"

Kire took his foot and pressed down on the platform again.

"With 170 South Pacific islands, many uninhabited, and most lined in white beaches and coral reefs, covered with tropical rainforest, Tonga is one of the most sought after vacation spot in the world."

He lifted his foot and the wall went white again.

Zeriakle sighed. "Ok, that's a place to start." He looked over at Nondukoma. "Uriel?"

"I see it. The people who helped her. They used this."

"So, just regular people?"

"They were. They're the ones who took her to the hospital. They're the ones who told us she was dead."

"Any more? Prophecies, anything?"

"Well. It's a big mess. I mean, what are we even trying to do anymore?" Nondukoma looked around for a chair. Seeing none, he sat on the floor.

"What do you mean, First of all we're trying to stay alive."

"We've been alive for so long already. Maybe it's time to just let someone else take over. I mean. That's what Aya wanted."

"And he got what he wanted. Look, I don't make the rules. When God dies, his angelic host dies, too. And the next god anoints new host. We did what we had to do to survive that." Zeriakl ws really not much happier about it than he was.

"So we align ourselves with Lucy? Is that who we are, really?"

"For a few thousand years, sure. Before this Emma Jackson gets too strong, we take her off the board, he gets chaos, it's a mess for a while, then we come in and line it all up. It'll be better. And we'll be alive."

Kire sighed. "Hey, how many islands did that thing say again?"

Ninety four islands later, Zeriakl, Nondukoma, and Kire appeared in blue flames on the heated porch in front of an island villa in Tonga.

Zeriakle instantly realized this was a bad idea.

Night was falling, but the lights by the pool clearly illuminated three of the people from the wedding that had helped Emma Jackson. They were standing there, staring right at them, naked.

But there was something else. Zeriakl knew that Nondukoma could see it.

The brown girl began to run forward toward them. She was fast, grabbing a spear she raised herself up and sent it through Kire's chest hard enough to explode his body onto the grass.

Zeriakl could see her aspect as she turned to him.

They were screwed.

The black woman walked forward, filled with her aspect. The air went black around her and the grass died with every step as her hand locked seamlessly around Zeriakl's throat. His spirit began to rise up as his body was eaten by the black death flame. He rose up watching Nondukoma there, alone now, to face the last man.

Looking to his left he saw him. The Messenger's eyes went black and he opened his mouth, a sound echoing out to tear through Nondukoma's flesh.

They weren't ready. How could they have missed this. Zerakl's spirit settled behind the pool and watched the three naked combatants stand there, the dead grass on fire behind them.

The girl in the middle saw his spirit. Of course she did. Zeriakl slowly raised one arm and lifted his middle finger. He shouted out, "Go Fuck yourself, Azrael."

She looked right at his spirit form as his words reverberated in her head, until, suddenly, she lifted her right hand into a middle finger and addressed what the other two must have thought was empty space.

"And fuck you, too."

I See Dead People

Here's where everything got kind of fucked up, for me.

I grew up Muslim. But I'm not one of those practicing religion people. I could practice, but I'd never get good at it. You're supposed to "submit to the word of God," but i'm not really much of a submtter. I'm more a "dominate the conversation"er. I did all that without any innuendo.

So this part of the story is going to get a little weird.

"Hey, tiny person. Are you talking over there?" Brooklyn yelled from across the table.

"I was just sort of narrating this."

"Excuse me?" She threw a biscuit at me. It bounced off my head.

"She really doesn't have to sit way down there." Gia was making a little building out of tater tots. It was pretty livable, really.

"You talk to her. She keeps saying she doesn't want to waste table."

"Yeah, I don't know what that means."

"Are you guys talking about me?" Brook tried throwing another biscuit. It sailed past my head.

"That's the angel of vengeance, over there."

"All this is weird." I started this trying to explain the weirdness. I'm not doing a very good job. Again, remember the four words we discussed.

Brook brought her plate down and put it next to me. "What is up, fuckers?"

"Welcome to the cool kids area." Giana made a motion with her hands.

Brooklyn looked around the room, "The fuck is up with this table, Sunny. If I sit over there, I feel like we're in a Henry the Eighth biopic, If I sit here it's like we're in a prison mess hall."

"Yeah, this whole room is designed for shit." I can't emphasize enough what a terrible rich person I am.

"Who am I again?" Brooklyn was sobering up from last night. After we defeated those demons, we just started drinking. I woke up with her boob in my mouth, which meant we were really fucked up. But we still didn't put a dent in the alcohol supply in this place. After a nuclear apocalypse, you could stay here in a fully drunk state for about thirty years.

Gia fielded that one. "You are the Angel Michael. You are a guardian, fearless, angel of vengeance and battle."

"And I'm avenging you two?"

"On occasion, yes."

"I do sound like I should be a guy, though. Should I grow a mustache?"

"Yes. Immediately." Giana sounded like she had considered that already.

I flipped through the book. The three religions of the book, Judaism, Christianity, and Islam, all seemed to have a fairly consistent idea of what these angels were about. I never thought about it before, but it was sort of eerie how consistent they were.

"There are four archangels that kind of hang out. Like we do. Somehow, we are turning into them."

"I would look good with wings." Brooklyn mused.

Giana nodded. "I think we all would. I think wings give everyone a little, you know, snap."

I read out loud, "Mikal (Michael) is one of the four primary angelic Host in all three major Semitic religions, along with Jibreel (Gabriel), the messenger of God, Azrael, the Angel of death, and Israfil, who is sometimes interchangeable with Metatron…"

"The voice of god." Gia looked up and let her tater tot house stand on its own. "Ta-da".

"How did you know that?" I looked up from the book.

Gia popped a tater tot in her mouth. "Sunday School, little bitches."

"Oh, my god. Do I have to be religious now? I just took the name of the lord in vain." Brooky looked torn.

"My personal feeling is that taking the name of the lord is vain is when you say out loud you worship God and then you act like a piece of trash. Like when you put up prayers and then stop feeding children." At least that's what my mom had taught me.

"So how is death feeling today?" Brook grabbed a tater tot from Gia's plate.

"So you guys couldn't see him at all, then. When he flipped me the bird and called me Azrael?"

"Not at all."

"So, I definitely see dead people."

"And you can kill grass"

"That seems like a minor ability."

"That death grip could come in handy."

"It was crazy. I just felt like I could do it. Like I could take all his energy. I'm the angel of death."

"Just like I knew that I could yell like that. That it was an aspect of the messenger."

"Who is the fourth one?" Brooklyn shoveled a forkful of eggs into her mouth.

I confess that I'd been thinking about that since last night. How did this happen and were there others? What could make people suddenly become versions of ancient angels. I did have one idea. I turned on the hologram of Veridian.

"That's the superhero from Manhattan."

"Only, what if she's not a superhero, either? What if she's an angel, too."

"Do you think she's Metatron?"

I had considered that. I didn't think so. "Well, she flies, like all of us. But she can grow things, communicate with animals and heal."

"And that doesn't sound like Metatron, does it?"

"No, but listen to this," I flashed the text on the table from my phone. "A powerful figure who guides the elements and ensures the balance of the environment. She heals, and is responsible for growing and healing flora, plants, and animals."

"That's pretty on the nose." Brooky moved on to my plate. This would be the time of the meal for that. I pushed it over to her.

Giana was fascinated, "Which one is that?"

"It's the angel Ariel."

There was a pause. I heard Brooklyn crunching.

"Like the Little mermaid?"

That did seem a bit of a let down. Until Giana stood up.

"Holy shit. I recognize her. And so do you guys."

I looked at the hologram. I still couldn't see it.

"Look at her mouth. She has kind of a bitch face. You just can't see the hair."

"What hair?"

"The brown and blonde streaks."

"Fuck."

"It's the nurse." I could see it now. The nurse at the hospital.

Brooklyn could see it, too, "Holy shit. That can't be a coincidence, can it?"

"So we all try to save this woman, Emma, and we bring her to the hospital. We're now becoming angels. And the first Nurse who works on her is turning into an angel, too."

"That tracks." Giana closed her eyes and put her hands on her hips. This is what she always did when she was thinking.

"Ok, So the people who touched Emma Jackson to save her became Angels. Including the Nurse who touched her."

"Right."

"So three guesses who metatron is."

Danny had never had a hostage situation quite like this. He looked out and saw at least twenty cars from every single facilitator group in a row in front of the Clinic.

"Is this like the most important vet clinic in the world?"

"Excuse me?" This was Vanessa's first situation like this. It looked just like it did in the movies.

Vanessa has an open and ordinarily happy face, sitting under a mop of curly black hair she had inherited from her Italian father, with the sleek light freckled skin of her Jamaican mother. She looked like someone who belonged outside. Just not here.

Danny sighed. "Walk me through this. Scumbag is holding a dog hostage. Every facilitator in the Triburrow area shows up. I get called in to negotiate, even though I'm technically off and I'm now being paid triple overtime. Is this a faberge dog or something?"

"It's the mayor's dog. I know that. He's cute. I know that. I follow him on social media." Vanessa held up her phone.

Reggie the dog had four million followers.

"Wow. Fuck me. Can you get me a line in there?"

"We got the phone number of the head groomer"

"Close enough. Light it up."

In the clinic, Tim leaned against the counter staring at Darcy. Darcy looked very much like he needed a bath. He held Reggie in his arms, a small red haired terrier who looked unaffected by what was happening as though he didn't realize that Darcy held a gun to his head or that Darcy had a general disdain for canine life.

Around the room, various dog owners sat holding their dogs. A combination of fear and abject confusion swam around the room. Who holds a dog hostage? That was a nightmare no one had bothered to have yet.

Tim's phone rang.

"Hey. I thought I said we're on do not disturb, Fucksock?" Darcy waved the gun angrily.

Tim pulled his hair back and fished for his phone in his front pocket. It continued to ring.

"Hey, Cuntface, Can you shut that fucking thing up?"

"This isn't a normal ring, man. I think it's the facilitators. You need to bargain…"

"I just need you to pay me or I take out internet dog, Cumspit. Comprende?"

"Look, we can't do that. We don't have any money here. We're just grooming internet dog…"

"His name is Reggie." interrupted one of the girls sitting on the floor.

"What?" Tim looked over at her.

Another girl answered, "Yeah, that's Reggie. I follow him, too."

A litany of responses rose up. An older man raised his hand, "he's my favorite."

Darcy nodded, "you tell me you have nothing? How much is this fucking dog worth?"

Tim sighed, "We're just grooming him."

"I will fuck you in the tit with that fucking phone. TURN IT OFF."

"I can't, man. It's the police. They want to talk to you." He tried to hand the phone to Darcy.

"Hey, balloon knot. Do I look like a man with a free hand right now? Just answer it, shit for dick."

"Soho Animal Clinic, Shit for dick speaking."

Danny had heard worse. "Is this Tim, the head groomer?"

"You know I am. With whom do I have the pleasure of speaking?"

Tim held his hand over the phone. "It's the facilitators. I think they like you."

Darcy waved him on. Go ahead, talk. "Tell them I want 30 million dollars and a car out of here or I put this legwarmer in the microwave and shove this gun up your dickhole."

"Did you hear that?" Tim hoped he wouldn't have to repeat it.

"Got it. Yeah. We can't do any of that."

Tim nodded, "cool, cool. Cool."

Darcy spit on the floor. "What did they say, Pissbitch?"

"Ok, his name is Danny, which is cool. It's kind of the boy version of your name."

"Are you messing with me, Fabio? I will fuck you in the eyeflap."

"Got it. So Darcy thanks you in advance for sending all that stuff. In the meantime, before the car gets here, we just need some pizzas."

"Hey, shitcrack. I didn't ask for Pizzas."

"If we feed the people in here, they will relax a little and not think you're going to kill everyone here."

"I AM going to kill everyone here."

Tim put the phone down, covering it up. "Sure. but LATER, after you get what you want, right?"

"Are you shitting me, Fistfuck?"

"Deep breath, man. You'll have your money and be on your way, we'll all be dead in a pool of blood and pizza crust and you can watch the pay for view movie later on Netflix.

Darcy stood there and looked at him. He tried to figure him out but he couldn't. Who the fuck was this kid?

The phone buzzed. "Hey. are we talking?" Danny was getting nervous."

"Can you let me know when those pizzas are here?" Tim covered the phone "Anyone here vegetarian?"

A spray of hands went up.

Tim lifted the phone to his ear, "Maybe just plain."

Darcy waved the gun. "Hey, kid, come over here."

"I got to go. Conference"

Danny put the phone down and turned to Vanessa, "can you get that place there to just leave a shitload of cheese pizzas on the stoop."

"Is that all?"

"For now. This guy's like a grenade with a third grade education. We may just need to take him out when he grabs the pizzas."

"Ok. give me 2 minutes. It's all set up."

Danny shook his head. "Darcy."

Darcy pulled Tim back behind the counter. "Look, man. You're kinda fruity but you don't seem like a bad guy."

"Well. thank you."

"I just need to get this money, right? But here's the thing, you fucking butt itch. I'm not going back to jail."

"Back to jail. There we go."

"And I will fucking eat this dog before that happens again. I will fucking put his hairy ass face in my mouth and eat him like a wonton, if you fuck me. Then I'll shoot your fucking dick off and eat that for desert. I don't care. I could use the fucking calories."

"Eat my dick. You're not going back to jail. Understood."

"Fucking right."

"Got it."

"See. We're communicating."

The phone buzzed. Tim looked at his messages.

"The pizzas are here. Ok. i can go wth you. We'll get them and bring them back in here."

"Wait. What the fuck, assboner. I'm not going anywhere."

"Well, ok. I thought you wanted to show them you really have the gun and stuff so they don't just... No worries."

"Wait. right. I go out there. You cover me. Like a shield."

"Right. I shield you. I try to make myself as big as possible. You grab the pizzas and we go back in."

"No fucking way. You grab the pizzas. You can do that and protect me at the same time, dicklotion."

"Ok. I guess if you leave the dog at the door, you can have the gun, I'll grab the pizzas and you shut the door-like slam it so they know you're serious."

"Yea. ok. Don't fuck with me. Do it exactly like that. Or I will shoot you in the fucking pisshole"

"Ok. Do you want to count down?"

"No, I don't fucking want to count down. What the fuck.Just move it, shit ticket.

Tim and Darcy slowly moved to the front of the clinic.

Darcy dropped Reggie right next to the door. Had he been a cat, Reggie would have flipped elegantly and landed on his feet from the three foot drop. But he was a dog so he fell clumsily onto his back and laid there like that, preserving energy and maybe maintaining some hope that someone might walk by soon and rub his belly.

They walked out on the stoop and Tim bent down to pick up the pizzas.

Danny watched, wondering exactly what was going on. "He put the dog down and now he's standing there waiting for us to shoot him."

"Yep."

"And the groomer guy is casually picking up pizzas, bending over and giving us space to just shoot this fucking guy right in the eye."

"It looks that way."

"Oh, fuck. Just have your people shoot this guy."

"Wait, look." Vanessa pointed to the stoop. Tim stood up holding the pizza precariously in one hand. He flashed them a finger."

"What does that mean? Wait a minute?"

"Or does it mean "up?"

"Why would it mean "up?"

At that moment, Tim grabbed the gunman and shot into the air at what looked like about a hundred miles an hour, sending the pizzas flying all over the parking lot in front of the clinic.

Danny watched them fly upward until they were a tiny dot.

"Welp. I guess it meant up"

Vanessa pulled out a pair of binoculars and handed them to Danny. He waved her on.

"You don't want to see?"

"I don't want to be the one to write this report. You look."

Vanessa took a deep breath. She really didn't want to fill this report out, either. In all honesty, she never wanted to be a facilitator. She loved painting birds and she knew that if she could get home before dark, there would be something beautiful to paint right outside her back window. She didn't care that much about perpetrators and honestly, if you pressed her, would have to admit that most people, to her, were just obstructions standing in front of an attractive bird.

All over Manhattan, right now, people were standing right in front of birds, thinking that they were in the right place. Exactly zero percent of them were. This Tim guy, honestly, the best thing he did today was to get out of the way and let her look at a fucking bird.

She lifted the binoculars and looked upward in a different direction. There were over thirty nine species of warbler indigenous to Manhattan and Vanessa had seen five of them before Tim came back down.

He dropped Darcy in a small green area by the entry of the Clinic. Darcy huddled and clutched the ground. He was crying and not moving much.

Tim pulled his hair up behind him and tied it up with a strand of his own hair. Danny thought to himself that it was a neat trick. The flying, too, was neat, but give credit where it's due. Hair is hard.

Vanessa slipped the binoculars into her pocket and stepped over to Tim with Danny.

She looked up at him as he handed her the gun. "You ok?"

He looked around. "Yep."

Danny was trying to figure out how to approach this. "So, that was cool. We were just going to shoot that guy."

"Yeah, that was my plan, too. You know, lead him out, let you shoot him."

They looked over at the gunman. He was still crying, cringing from being touched.

"Yeah, this is probably better."

"Yeah."

Vanessa figured she would be the one to ask. "So, how'd you, uh, you know, fly like that?"

Danny folded his arms. He was curious as well, provided he didn't need to fill out a report.

"You know I just felt like I could do it. Kind of out of nowhere. And it worked."

"It did. What happened up there?"

"Oh, I just flew him around, took the gun. Talked."

Darcy was screaming and crying. He fell to the ground and rolled over shaking.

"Jesus. What did you say?"

"Oh, to him?"

Tim looked at Darcy.

"I told him what God thought about him.

Be Careful what you wish for

Emma Jackson stepped through History.

Unfortunately, History wasn't always kind to footwear. She lifted her foot. Moving over to the grass, she wiped it off. It made a bigger mess. She kicked off her shoes.

She thought that she might regret that later.

The edge of the sky almost seemed to taper its brilliant blue to a serene aqua before meeting the verdant green hills. But all that was in the distance. All that was so far away. The town she stepped through was empty, each house looking as though it were just built, pristine, modern, comfortable. This was a new development.

Emma was more interested in its past. She waved her hand.

The streets were full of people dying, diseased, carrying limp bodies of dead children. Homes were nailed shut, the sound of desperation filled the streets.

She moved forward, following a young mother carrying her dying infant. A voice stopped her.

"You know, there isn't anything good in that direction."

"I know that. Good's not what I'm looking for."

She turned and saw Aya standing behind her. His face looked exactly as it did in that hotel room. But he had now draped a modern white suit over his lanky frame. It seemed to fit him poorly.

"West Cork Ireland. The Potato Famine. There are beautiful places to see in Ireland. I would recommend Kilarney National Park."

"Yeah, I saw pictures of that when I was a kid. Beautiful."

"Yes, you did. I'm probably going to be short on new information. I am dead, after all."

"I know."

The scene changed around her. Suddenly, they were on an island, filled with thatched huts and tribal markets, European and Colonial traders dragged African men and women around cruelly. A group were herded off to a ship."

Aya shook his head. "Gorée Island. At one point, there were twenty eight different slave trading houses operated by white people, moving enslaved people to the "new world." This is like a greatest hits."

"Not greatest."

"What are you trying to see?"

"It's the issue of Theodicy, isn't it? From ethics class. How could a god allow this? All benevolent, all seeing, all powerful."

"Allow? That's a lesson to learn, I think. No one allows anything. People take. People want. No one allowed this, not me, not anyone. Some people wanted. And they got what they wanted."

"That doesn't seem very just."

"Again, I'm a figment of your imagination, Emma. So expect no new information from me."

"The people who want the hardest win?"

"Want, Wish, make, hurt, create, etc. What we bring into the world is the only thing that matters. Talk is nothing. It's hoping people will change their minds. Nothing changes what's been done."

"It's ugly. It's beneath us." She shielded her eyes from the cruel African sun.

"Nothing is beneath us, except the earth. Are you familiar with the experiments of Philip Zimbardo, and Stanley Milgram?"

"Clearly. You are."

"Ha. Right. Give us power and we use it like a magnifying glass in the sunlight, charring insect wings because we had that they can fly. Tell us we CAN and we hear that we HAVE TO."

"Those experiments were white students, steeped in white culture. Did you know that? They were a chapter in this, what you see all around you. That human cruelty that was fostered so that people could be a part of THIS. "

The setting moved to Virginia. A building was being built by enslaved people. A white overseer beat a young man over and over.

"Notaway County, Virginia. At one point, the population was seventy four percent enslaved people. So few others." Emma stared into the distance.

Aya stepped in front of her. "And that rest wanted."

"And God does nothing."

"If you don't mind me fast forwarding, I'm guessing, but...next up."

The scene changed to a Nazi concentration camp.

"March, 1933, Dachau, not far from beautiful Munich. The very first of nearly 44,000 camps and other incarceration sites designed to solve the 'jew problem'"

The scene unfolded around her. It was devastating to look at.

"Where were you? While all of this was happening?"

"What do you want to hear? I'm still a figment of your imagination. Do you think that God can stop people determined beyond reason to hurt each other? SHOULD he? Is it the job of a god to kill Hitler in his crib, or to slow inflation?"

"I don't know. I don't know what the job is."

"Neither did I, Emma. I just wanted someone good to be doing it. Even if all they were doing was standing to testify."

Emma walked up to Aya. She looked at his face, just as she remembered. She said to herself as much as to him, "I think we have to do better than that."

The concentration camp behind them vanished.

The scene shifted to a motel, right outside New York. Emma walked through the parking lot and stopped at the pop machine. She looked down and realized she wasn't wearing any shoes. She touched the pop machine and a slot appeared, right above the Grape soda one. It held a pair of black comfortable flats. She pressed the button and the shoes fell to the opening. Reaching in she pulled them out and slid them on.

She turned and began walking to a room. Then she stopped.

Back to the machine, she hit the grape soda button twice, grabbing the sodas from the opening as they fell.

Then she moved on to the room.

She knocked on the door to room 4a, on the ground, just around the corner. It was sunny and beautiful. The door swung open and Betina screeched, pulling her inside.

She hugged her, "I thought you were gone. By the time I got to the hospital, they said you checked out but you were in bad shape. I came by and couldn't find you. I fell asleep in front of your door. Where did you go?"

Emma pet her hair, "It's ok. I'm fine. I'm ok. I'm here."

"Em, I'm so sorry."

"What are you sorry about?"

"I got so freaked out. I Just hid. I was so drunk and I just hid.

"It's ok, baby. I got you. Look." She pulled apart and handed a grape soda to Betina.

"Drinks are on me today."

"Isn't this sweet?" Aya stood by the door, behind Betina. Clearly she couldn't hear him. Emma shot daggers at him.

"Thank you. Come sit down. What are you doing? Where did you go?"

"What are you doing here, baby girl?"

"Right." She sat on the edge of the bed. "After you went to the hospital, I freaked out and tried to sober up and get down there. I finally found the hospital they had taken you to but you had already checked out. I just couldn't go home."

"Yeah, I got the hell out fast."

"I'm so sorry."

"You have nothing to be sorry for."

"She kind of does." Aya leaned up against the desk. He folded his arms. Emma waved him off.

"I didn't do anything to help. I wish I did."

"Girl, you were drunk."

"I was."

"I tell you what. If you think you did anything wrong. I forgive you."

The floodgates went off and Betina was overcome with tears.

Emma rocked her back and forth. Over her shoulder, Emma took a drink from her can of soda.

"It's so good to see you."

"You, too, girl."

"So. What are you here for? What can I do for you?"

"Bet, can I tell you a secret?"

"Of course. Anything."

Emma touched her hand and they both felt a spark

"You're ok with secrets?"

"Absolutely."

Emma looked at her. Betina was such a pretty girl. And they were so different in so many ways. What a strange world that would pull them together like this. But, there, in that room, they were so similar. They were so connected. Emma took a big swig of her grape soda.

"I think I'm hallucinating."

Zeriakl, Nodukoma, and Kire appeared in the middle of a starkly white room.

"Oh, fuck me." Zeriakl put his head in his hands.

Nondukoma took a breath. "Ok, we regroup. It's good."

"Spread, fuckheads." Kire looked down to see Peabody holding what looked like a giant q-tip.

"I don't…. Where does that even go?"

Zeriakl kicked at the small demon. "We just need to see Lucy."

"Hey. Get Sudsy, bitches."

"We don't - "

The room filled with a massive, unstoppable wave of bleach and water again, buffetting them around. Kire tried to just go with the flow this time. He let himself sink underwater. It was just easier this way. About a minute later, when they found themselves in the red room, lying on the floor, Kire realized that letting go made it easier for him. He felt at peace. He closed his eyes and slowly sat, legs crossed. He was clean. He was purified.

"What's his deal?" Lucifer threw a spoon at Kire. He sat at a long red table with the other demons flanking him.

Zeriakl sighed. "He's coping."

Satan took a big bite, ripping meat from the bone. "You guys don't have the protection you used to. I mean, sure, you can spawn here, but nobody's stopping anyone from kicking your ass."

"We get it.

"You should try this."

"Yes, eat my ass."

In the middle of the table was a large, blob-like demon. His skin was roasted, much like the red colored roasted pork in Chinese restaurants. There were large cuts removed from his belly and back and a large swath missing from his flank. It matched the meat sitting on the plate.

"Eat my whole fucking ass."

Zeriakl looked back at Satan. "Who is that?"

Satan laughed. "That's fucking dinner, man. Here."

He dropped a couple slabs of meat on the plates in front of Zeriakl and Nondukoma.

"We appreciate you letting us sort of come together here before we get back to it." Nondukoma gingerly touched the meat.

"Oh, come on, eat."

"Dude, eat out my fucking ass, it's so fucking good. Oh yeah. "

"Can he not do that?"

"It's cool. Check it out." Satan picked up a slab of meat hanging from a bone."Hey, meat, I fucking love this on the bone." He licked it with his long red tongue and then inserted the bone right in his mouth. "I want to fucking choke on your meat. It's so fucking big." He took a giant bite and the Roasted Demon moaned.

"Oh yeah. Get that down your throat. Yeah. Fuckng suck it. Eat my bitch meat. Fuck me up."

"Do you guys want us to leave?" Zeriakl made a motion to stand up.

Satan looked over in confusion. "Why? - c'mon. Let's eat him at the same time."

He dug his face into his plate, licking up the juices and devouring the meat like an animal. "You fucking piece of meat. I love your meat juice, bitch, get your ass in my fucking mouth."

"Oh fuck, that's so good. Eat it. Chew that fucking bone. Suck my fucking meat. All of you, wreck my asshole, use me, c'mon. "

Kire opened an eye and considered standing up. It seemed to make more sense to hang out on the floor.

Currently, many of the other demons around the table were starting to get into it. If you were a judge of facial expressions you may have thought that all Zeriakle wanted at that point was for the thousand years of Chaos and Tribulation to be over already.

"Lick that shit up, you fucking animal - I want to shove my meat all the way down your throat. Ooooh."

If Nondukoma didn't know better, he would have thought the eviscerated carcass on the table was having an orgasm. Satan looked overjoyed. "I love a good meal."

Zeriakl figured he'd try to talk. "So we're not that strong without the protection of heaven and the host?"

"Nope." Satan made a big deal out of licking the juices from his dinner. "And I can't really protect you because you haven't really declared fealty to me. I can give you a place to spawn, out of professional courtesy."

Nondukoma spoke up, "And we appreciate that a lot."

"I mean, I wish you were more fun." Satan slid down the table to where the roasted demon was and reached his fist in to pull out a chunk of meat.

"Oh, fuck, that's right. Get up there and rip out that fucking meat. I'm such a fucking pig for you." The roasted demon's eyes rolled back into his head in pleasure.

"We want to kick off this thousand years," Zeriakl tried to catch Satan's attention.

"Yeah, that would be hot. Chaos on earth. I mean, I won't be there." He reached over and was handed a towel. He wiped his hands off. "Fucking petri dish of a planet. But I'll get you guys. You can rip it up."

Zeriakl stood up and moved toward Satan. He was a hard guy to figure out. "What do you want after all this?"

Satan laughed, which, in turn, triggered a round of laughter all around the room. "Don't worry about me." He put his arm around the Blue-black demon, "I'm always going to be ok."

He slapped Zeriakl on the back. "You know you got a window." Zeriakl looks confused.

"This new God?" Satan leaned in conspiratorially. "She thinks she's crazy."

It's really hard to come up with coherent reasons to leave Tonga. I say this as I write on a holoscreen that is floating above a large hot tub looking over an immense drop to a particularly beautiful piece of the pacific ocean, an area so remote that this entire area of the earth just looks blue from space.

Yes, there were a few giant inflatable dinosaurs on the side of the hot tub, but that's because, even in the most beautiful place on earth, we are small children. We had bought those a year ago, the first time we all came here, and graded each other on how well we could fuck them. So judge away, everybody.

Brook and I are simmering in water that would have been entirely too hot for us a week ago while Giana floats about six feet above us naked, in a cross legged Buddha pose. If you can't paint that picture in your head, this means that we can see everything that God ORIGINALLY gave her if we look up. And that seemed to be all Brooky wanted to do.

"That's a magnificent pussy." she said, hypnotized.

"Thank you." Gia was falling in and out of some kind of trance, too.

Brook looked over at me. "I mean, It's like a painting. it's flawless."

"What kind of flaws would pussies have?" I wasn't exactly a gold star homosexual, but my experiences had mostly been with Brook when she felt like ordering me around. I was sort of her Dinosaur sometimes. Once she made me donk her from behind saying shitty things about her ex to make her feel better. That's not going in either one of our memoirs and I'm not proud of it, but spend enough time with people and shit gets wiggly.

"Mostly none. Pussies are perfect. Penises are weird. Yours is sort of weird."

I couldn't even fight that. My experience with Penises were varied and complex. And my own can't really be depended on, to be honest, to not be weird.

"Should I start to call you Michael from now on? I think it's kind of cool and genderbendy."

"I don't mind it." She looked up at Gia, "Can you find him?"

Gia looked over, "I think he has to be close to death for me to locate him. But I'm seeing all these people, all over the planet, who are on the verge of death. It's powerful."

She floated down a bit until she was just hovering over the water. "On that note, make sure no Dinosaurs fall into this. They'd be soup pronto. It's like 200 degrees, you fucking radioactive monsters."

"Oh, is it?" I turned the temperature up another five degrees. It was really bracing. I couldn't help but notice I wasn't dying. Also, I wasn't pruning up.

"What do you have to do for the dying people?"

"That's what I'm trying to figure out. We don't really have a manual here. I wish we did."

"That wouldn't suck."

I had been thinking about this since we had originally made the angel connection. I was about to say something that made me sound smart.

I did love those moments.

"So, When that woman, Emma was being attacked, I was thinking about looking at every part of it so I could report it, write about it. I was just being me. Sort of the messenger."

Giana nodded. She seemed to get where this was going. "Brook stood up and defended her."

Brook raised her hand, "I tried to. Not too successful."

Giana lifted a hand, "and then, she died in my arms. In a way."

"At the hospital, that Nurse worked to heal her."

"And at that same hospital, StevenTim carried her and checked her in." Giana continued.

"He spoke for her." This was only really making sense if the elephant in the room was cleared up.

"So, what are we saying?" Brook pulled herself up from the sunken hot tub. I couldn't help but notice she didn't really need a towel anymore. She grabbed a Dinosaur and began riding it back to the house.

"You go, you crazy bitch."

She fell over and laid there with the Dinosaur between her legs. Giana grabbed one of the other ones and jumped on her.

"Dinosaur Attack!"

I grabbed the two remaining Dinos and threw them down on them. I wonder if this would have kept them from extinction. Just a little fucking fun every once in a while.

I fell on the ground next to them and looked up. "Are we saying that we think Emma Jackson is God?"

Giana rolled over and looked at me. "Why would she be pretending to be a normal human?"

"Ooh, ooh, I know this." Brook tried to get on top and ride a dino. "I read this story in grade school about God- Boy god, I guess- who walked the earth one day every year as a human being. Just to see what's up."

"Cool story, Bro," Giana rode her Dinosaur over to her and tackled her. Brook got back up and rode furiously, "I am the Dinosaur of Vengeance."

I threw the two remaining Dinos at them. Let them battle.

Giana reared up, naked and insane, on her Dinosaur, "All of you are like nothing compared to my Dinosaur might." She flexed her muscles in the night air rising up to her full height.

Just as she did, the automatic lights around the house went on. I didn't realize how dark it was. The shock of light was overwhelming. And then, a silhouette came walking out of the glare and stood staring at us. I rubbed my eyes.

It was StevenTim in a pair of jeans and a black t-shirt.

"How the fuck did you guys get all the way out here?"

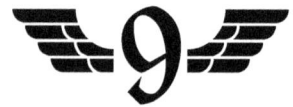

How to Teleport in a Few Easy Steps

StevenTim had been explaining to us what his abilities were while we all played a giant game of Jenga at the breakfast table. We had originally explained that we had teleported here, but it looks like he wasn't really conversant with modern advancements in teleportation. And neither was his friend, the pretty curly haired girl with the entertained look on her face. Next to her, he seemed overly serious.

"My name is just Tim."

"Why are you reading over my shoulder? I'm writing this for me." I stuck my tongue out at him.

"It's just... It's just Tim, ok?"

"These are your people?" Vanessa cocked her head, making sure to stick closely by Tim's side. "They don't seem like you kind of people."

"I went on a tinder wedding date with her" He pointed to Giana, the only one of us intent on winning the game. She waved and the floppy white rope she had put on over her slipped down, exposing her boobs.

"She's hot, nice match." Vanessa laughed.

Giana wrapped herself back up appreciatively, "Thank you, girl."

Vanessa looked at Tim, "A wedding date? First date from a Tinder match?"

Tim shook his head, "Not my idea." Gia raised her hand sheepishly.

Brooky stood up as Gia knocked massive jenga pieces everywhere. They were like the size of baseball bats. "So, you could sort of zone in on us?"

Tim looked at Brooky, "Yeah, I meditated and it seemed like I just knew where you were. Then I just had to get here."

"Gia tried to do that but she couldn't find you because you aren't dying."

"Yeah. If you really liked me you would be a little dying."

Vanessa looked at her and smiled, "Yes, men really need to show more effort sometimes."

Gia cocked her head to one side and put her hand over her heart. "Oh, I love her."

"You can only find people if they are near death?" Tim ignored it all.

"Or dead, apparently. I see dead people. I'm like 1999 Bruce Willis with boobs."

"And you were able to teleport here?"

I spoke up, "Yes, my family has credits. I never use them. I'm a terrible rich person."

Tim looked around. He didn't disagree. He also didn't seem that interested in Jenga. He walked around the room. For some reason he seemed more pensive than he had at the wedding. They remembered him being a little more, well, fun.

Giana got up and grabbed a banana from off the counter. She peeled it and ate it. "We have a theory that Emma Jackson is God."

Tim nodded. He was quieter, more introverted. "She is."

Vanessa broke in, "He thinks she is."

"I do."

"Where is she now?" Brook asked.

"She's with a friend. If I close my eyes I can almost see her."

That was curious to me. "So, Just Tim can see God and we can't?"

"He is Metatron, the voice of God?" Vanessa seemed like she was trying it out- to see if she believed it.

"Which is not one of the transformers?" Brook offered.

"Strangely, no."

I couldn't quite figure out what Vanessa's relationship was to Tim. She looked protective of him.

"So how do you guys know each other?"

"We actually just met a few days ago. At the Dog Clinic." Tim was dismissive, but I suspected there was a bigger story there by the look on Vanessa's face.

"I'm a facilitator."

To back track a little, by 2088, there were no police anymore. The idea of people barging into situations with guns and taking control was seeming less and less productive. They were uniformly replaced by facilitators which were sort of a cross between general problem solvers, rescue workers, and social workers. Some were specialized, like firemen and paramedics, but most were sort of jack-of-all-trades helpers meant to figure out situations. From what I could figure out, Vanessa bonded with just Tim at some kind of crisis and was now trying to see it through. She seemed kind, as I imagined you'd have to be.

"I was also in catechism for about ten years, so maybe I can help a bit.

"We have extra dinosaurs, so..." Brook removed a jenga piece that should have caused a disaster. It did not.

Gia padded over to Just Tim and stood on her toes to see into his face.

She had pulled out her phone. "You know, you could have found me more easily. I never unmatched you on Tinder."

'Damn, really?"

"And I owe you ten thousand dollars." I chimed in,

Gia pointed at me, padding back to the table, "yep"."

"Yeah, and did you guys fly all the way here?"

Tim looked at Vanessa. "Oh, I was going to but…"

He disappeared in a flurry of blue flame, reappearing across the room, behind me the same way. "That's why I wanted to see, uh."

I swiveled and knocked over Giant Jenga. That was a pretty cool display.

"Oh, yeah. Let me show you the teleporters."

The invention of material teleportation in 2067 was as purely accidental as any scientific discovery can be. To understand it, you may first need to know the things that led up to it.

The first was ongoing research into quantum teleportation. This is a way of teleporting information across distances instantly. In this case, instantly means faster than the speed of light. It requires something called quantum entanglement. Which is not a split ends hair problem.

It is something that happens when two particles link together in a certain way no matter how far apart they are in space. Their state remains the same.

So, for example, you're having dinner one day and there just happens to be a decaying pi meson on the table.

Yes, you should clean better.

As you eat, it breaks down and expels an electron and a positron.

The two particles are entangled because their spins must add up to the spin of the pi meson.

Observing one particle's spin reveals the other particle's spin no matter how far apart they are. So if one particle goes off to college to meet a nice girl and I pass the information of the other to a third particle, I have passed that distant particle's information to it faster than information could have organically arrived spanning that distance.

And quantum teleported that information.

This was the path most teleportation researchers were on. Everything is just information, right? No one will argue that if we're just talking about a chicken sandwich. Despite the ongoing battle between Popeyes and KFC, a chicken sandwich is fungible, one is fundamentally the same as any other identical one.

With humans, we have some nits to pick. One is called the myth of continuity. Historically, philosophers referred to it as the Ship of Theseus paradox.

Theseus was the son of a god who once famously slew a half man-half bull creature called the Minotaur. This gives you some idea of the general historicity of this, by the way.

At any rate, he hopped on his ship and came home, famously. Every year, to celebrate that, his people would take that ship, out up in a museum until that day every year, and recreate that journey. Of course they needed to replace a rudder here, a plank here, a wheel here, etc. So, after hundreds of years, when each part had been replaced more than once, was it still the ship of Theseus?

Continuity is about identity. If I use the INFORMATION of you and rebuild you on the other side, is that really YOU? If it's put together just like you but the material is different, is it you?

Tough one, Especially if you start to factor in ephemerals like souls.

So, maybe not the exact path.

Turning people into energy, sending them over a line, then turning them back had some of the same problems. Added to those, though, was now the issue that turning things to energy and back seemed to require massive explosions - the kind that humans rarely survived.

Since the world had been experimenting with warp drive technology, the obvious angle may have been wormholes. Strap someone into a device, open a wormhole to somewhere else, shove them through it. That seemed reasonable. More and more, though, it looked like wormholes would be unstable and dangerous for a long time in the future. Making one, going through one, getting rid of one, they all had challenges. Some of which included those explosions we discussed above.

Humans and explosions didn't mix well.

The problem was solved in a way that seemed extremely counterintuitive. It was called Phase-Kinesis teleportation.

Let's break the teleportation problem down to three problems. To teleport an actual object, you need to:

1. Make the object you want to teleport capable of passing through the objects in between the origination and the destination.

2. Make the object you want to teleport capable of traveling faster than normal material objects

Leaving you free to:

3. Accelerate the object from the origination point to the destination point and then slow it back down.

To start with, Atoms are primarily empty space. We think of matter as solid, but it's not. What makes a brick solid is not the number of particles in there but the push and pull of the electric fields between the particles.

If you drop that brick on the floor, it is stopped from going through the floor basically because of the electric repulsion felt by the electrons in the atoms in the brick due to the presence of the electrons in the atoms of the floor and not because of the density of the particles or the lack of available space for the electrons to move through.

What if we could temporarily overcome those electric forces between the atoms. We could "Phase" the brick through the floor. This accomplishes number 1.

Scientists in England had come up with a way to turn materials into a new form of matter for milliseconds. The new matter form was called "phase receptive matter" and it happened when the forces between the particles were disabled for a very short period of time. Phased matter immediately lost its mass and acted like a series of linked massless particles, maintaining the connections, but not the behaviors of those forces.

So that helped with number 2. As a massless series of particles, phased matter could effectively pretend to be a bunch of photons. And photons naturally traveled at the speed of light.

Now chase number three. You just turned a brick into something that acted like light for a tiny fraction of a second. This kind of "light" could penetrate any object.

Now, some researchers at the University of Maryland had come up with a device they just called a "light gun." It basically used the existing satellite network to send beams of light anywhere on earth, wherever people needed illumination for a short period of time. They broke off from the university and started a company called "GLOW" in 2065 that could send a coherent light field anywhere you wanted so, if you lost your keys, you'd be all good.

That company failed.

But the light gun was a hit. In fact, they named the company LIGHTGUN™.

So let's say you want to teleport from point A to point B. The teleport system first has to send a particle scanner that can penetrate the ceiling and walls of point B without punching a hole in it. The entire path from Point A to point B is charted perfectly, triangulated, using existing satellites. No, you or the object you need teleported undergoes the procedure to become phase receptive matter.

This happens so fast that no one knows. Your particles don't even have time to drift apart. The light gun then "shoots" you to point B where mirrors and opaque surfaces stop you. No mass, no inertia. You instantly revert back to classical matter.

You are composed of the EXACT SAME PARTICLES.

You are only immaterial for a fraction of a second. Remember, light can circle earth 7.5 times in one second, getting a body from Manhattan to one of the islands of Tonga, for example takes way way less than that.

You experience no effects from the travel.

Now, as you can imagine, turning someone into a massless phase and shooting them at a teleport receiver took years to perfect. Many bricks were lost in that research. And it costs a fortune to do it. The first few trips cost over a billion dollars each. But now that it's been perfected, the process is used all over the world by the extremely rich, mostly to make it to Gala openings that they would otherwise be uncomfortably late to.

"What if I don't want to do this with you?" Gia pulled her long striped socks on under her robe. We were all going to get dressed very slowly, probably taking much of the day. I was still naked under my robe.

"I thought you could just use the teleporters you have, but that's so expensive. I don't know why I can teleport and you can't. Flying around to do this is not viable, i think. I think you need me."

Tim seemed to be taking to this angel thing better than the rest of us.

"I don't mean I don't want to hang out with you. I mean I don't want to flitter all over and fucking kill people."

"You're not going to be killing people."

"That's what I do now, right? I'm the angel of death."

"I think you need a whole new black wardrobe." Brook offered.

Gia waved her hand. "Even that part I hate. I have dark skin. I look really good in bright colors."

Sitting on the sidelines, I had to admit that this was true. She had a yellow sundress that she wore all the time last summer that made guys go crazy.

Tim looked frustrated. "Obviously I'm not trying to control what you wear, but I'm just saying, I can come with you and help. I'm seeing this list of people, too.

Vanessa looked curious, "What is this list?"

Gia was as animated as I'd ever seen her. "The list of people who are dying. Or who are dead and don't realize it and need to be sent off."

"That's brutal." Vanessa shivered.

"Thank you. This is who I am now, I guess and I didn't sign up for it."

"I know you didn't. I didn't, either, but these names and visions aren't going to stop. Maybe if we do this we can start to learn to manage it."

"You know this is going to be worse than our FIRST date?"

Tim finally laughed. "Look, I'm going to keep my shirt on the whole time."

Brook was eating an ice pop making this particular statement far worse. "I like him better topless, so this is already a bust."

"I was going to have sex with him after the wedding date, if the food was good."

"The food was so good. Those meatballs."

"That could have been an epic night."

Tim closed his eyes and shook his head, "Do you know what a psychopomp is?"

"No, I do not." Gia leaned back onto the table.

"In some cultures, they have psychopomps, who are mysterious creatures that help people understand that they are dead, assist them in moving on, make it easier for them to get to the other side and pass over.

You're saying Azrael is a psychopomp?"

"That is the tradition. It evolved out of the human realization that death is lonely, scary, terrifying, even. It's a time in your life when you feel the most confused, the most hopeless, the most without another person at your side. Some people say that the idea of the psychopomp is a kind of wish fulfillment. So people can not feel quite so lonely at the time when they know they'll need it the most.

"So I run around and visit people who are dying and help them pass over."

"Yes."

"And you know this because..."

"I am the voice of god?"

"Bullshit."

There was a thump at the glass and I saw, from the corner of my eye, a brightly colored splash against the door leading to the hot tub. When I made my way out the door I saw Gia and Brook running toward the body of a pretty little bird. It had a beautiful black face and a butt that was covered in red and orange feathers.

Gia kneeled down and picked him up. He looked close to death. She pet him delicately and he recoiled, as though in pain. Her eyes went black and she put her hands around him and drew him in to her chest,

She whispered,"It's ok, little guy.It's not your time yet." Putting the little bird inside her robe, she stood up.

Brooky followed her as she moved to the middle of the hard, their robes waving in the wind like white flags. Gia held up her hands and said a few more unintelligible things to the bird. She lifted him up and Brook cheered as the little guy launched itself into the sky. The bird shot upward about twenty feet, circled, and then dipped away to our right, disappearing in the distance.

"Be a little more careful, tiny dude," Brooky offered as he flew off and the two of them came back inside.

"I think he said his name was Henry Redbutt." she said to Gia.

"Of the Massachusetts Redbutts? What are the odds?"

Vanessa stood next to me watching. Her eyes were wide open. I leaned in.

"Just keep the doors open when you come back in. It's so nice here."

Tim was still in meditating pose. There was a list in his hands. He stepped down onto the ground as though he had been sitting on a tall chair. Vanessa walked over and stood by Gia. She leaned against her slightly as she looked at Tim.

"If you guys are doing this, I want to come with and help."

Sympathy for the devil

A long time ago, Lucy stood next to Aya as they watched the woman scratch lines into tree bark. She, in turn, was staring out watching some men wrestle in the dirt, fighting over what looked to be a small wild boar.

Lucy finally cheered when she finished writing. He let out a big hoot. She looked around as though she may have heard SOMETHING. She shrugged and went back to work.

"You are really into this writing stuff." Aya touched the words carved into the tree. They were raw and not deep. A few days of inclement weather would remove them, likely.

Lucy grunted, "hrh. Trust me, without this, we're going to spend the next couple thousand years watching people invent the same shit over and over again.

"I see your point." He patted him on the back. "This is why I rely on you, Metatron."

"Hey, I do what I can, little brother."

So we should probably stop there for a second and explain. Lucifer was Metatron? And he was God's big brother? That doesn't sound biblical at all. Although that's the kind of nepotism you might expect from a bureaucracy like this.

Twenty thousand years before this, Aya got up on a hill and danced, screaming out his pain, making his case that God was insufficient in the world.

That HE would be a better God.

And God, tired and ready to pass on the power that made them, well, god, said ok."

And made Aya the next god.

It took a while for Aya to understand that this was how the rules worked. He didn't realize he even WAS god.

The next few days were a blur. Lucy was only a few years older than Aya, and had been living a few miles away, in his own place. He made the trek back into the village to check on what his brother was doing.

And his brother was doing not well. The loss of his wife and oldest son sort of hammered the nail in his coffin. But his health was surprisingly good. Lucy took his little brother out hunting, over and over again, trying to get his mind off of it.

And, eventually, it sort of worked.

And when people in the town came to check in on him, Lucy was the one who spoke for him, answered for him. He tried to take care of him.

What neither Aya or Lucy knew at the time was that the universe had certain roles- specific jobs to hand out. One was the job of being GOD. And, without knowing, Aya had taken that job.

And one was the role of Metatron, the voice of god. And by supporting his little brother through it all, Lucy had taken THAT job.

And it stuck.

One day, Aya touched Lucy on the arm and Lucy's mind opened up.

He realized he could see, a bit, into Aya's head. He could visualize the world around him. He could lift large amounts. He could fly. He could teleport, appearing anywhere he wanted, even places he'd never been.

And he suddenly KNEW things. He understood the rules. He understood what he and Aya had turned into.

He knew what they had to do.

"So, you're just going to follow this woman around?" Aya asked, 20,000 years later.

"No. Well, yes, a bit. I just need to make sure nothing happens to her."

"Writing sounds like it's going to be a big hit."

"Not that anyone will remember her for it."

"That's sad. It's a good thing that the elders are going to decide to give her and her family that mammoth coat blanket. That'll be a good start."

"Oh, yeah?"

"Yep. Next week." Aya smiled at him.

Lucy put his arm around God. "You little sneak. Have I told you lately that I love you?"

"In the last 20,000 years? Yes. quite a few times."

"Has it been that long, already? Damn. It feels like only 10,000."

"It really doesn't."

"Nope."

Things were good between them for literally hundreds of thousands of years. That's really exponentially longer than most relationships last. Family is hard.

About 140,000 years ago, Aya and Lucy met in what would one day be called Agadir, Morocco, standing over a burned and desolate camp. They watched an old man walk through the thatched huts, carrying a small brown bag. He set it down and rested. This is where it started, probably.

Aya was clearly on edge. "So that's it, then. There he goes. Off to die. The last of us."

"Well, I mean, there are lots of OTHER people, other groups. You know."

"But our line. OUR people." It was true. This was the last of the subspecies of man that would one day become known as H. Bodoensis, the lineage that Aya and Lucy belonged to. This was the last of the thick ones.

"It IS a moment, for sure." Lucy tried to figure out why this was hitting Aya so hard. He had seen this coming.

"Maybe it's time for me to go, too. I hear petitions. People want the job."

"I'm sure they do. It's a good job. The hours suck."

"They do. But…"

"I see,. Look, we talked about this. If you want to step down…"

""I won't."

"You will. And you won't worry about me. Because that's not how all of this is supposed to work."

"You know the rules better than I do. You're the one that told me the rules."

"Aya, look. Look around you. This world is big. It's huge. The rules have allowed that there will always be a god and there will always be helpers.

And there will always be people that need things. We play our roles and then move on."

"What's this man's name?"

"Don't do this."

"What's his name?"

"His name is Gompa"

"That's a terrible name."

"It's a terrible name."

"Gompa?"

"Move on from that."

"He's not the last. When he goes. He's not." Aya came close to his brother and hugged him.

"You are."

The rules of the universe are unyielding. In science, we try to push them, to use them, to simulate breaking them to serve what we need.

But the rules persist.

And the rules of this universe? When God steps down and another god takes over, all of his helpers, his angels, well...

They step down as well.

They die.

It happens quickly. When Aya took over, the heavenly host that preceded him fell apart within twenty minutes. They all died. Except the ones that had rebelled.

Except the fallen.

And about 139,000 years ago, Lucy did it. He rebelled. Not because he didn't like the job, because in all honesty, he quite did. And not because, like Zeriakl, Nondukomo, and Kire, he wanted to safeguard his own life, even after the ascension of a new god.

But, instead, for a secret, third reason.

"So, what's it like?"

"Down there?"

"Down there."

Aya and Lucy met on a cliff in Sarakiniko Beach in what would be Milos, Greece, overlooking a beach bridging the cool untouched blue of the Aegean Sea with crystalline sand. The air carried droplets of seawater across the beach and upward, perfectly temperate and so clear that the water itself felt light, in the air, dreamlike, ephemeral.

It was beautiful.

Lucy's wings had turned wide and red. They glistened in the liquid air under the warm Greek sun. He turned to God.

"Ha. Life works differently there. It's not real, you know? No one really dies. So life is cheap. It's a game. That's it. The underworld is one big game."

"And you like it, now? Or what?"

"I don't like it, I don't Dislike it. It just is. I don't take it seriously. It's not to be taken seriously. Some souls show up for a little bit, try and figure out what they did wrong, try to learn a little something, then they move on. It's a way station. It's a gift shop.

"So you quit to work in the gift shop."

"Yes, I did. You can say that. I quit the nine to five to work at a toy store."

"I miss you, Lucy."

And I miss you, but you have Alegio. He's a good Metatron."

"He doesn't get my jokes."

"You're God, no one gets your jokes."

"You see, like that. That is deep. That is some deep shit and you just tossed it out. Alegio doesn't do that."

"Give him 100,000, years, Jeez. Let him ramp up a little. Let him work his way into the job. "

"You really piss me off."

"No, I don't. You're pissed off by how little I piss you off."

"Yes. And I'm pissed off that you know that."

"You know what I'm going to do?"

"Give some more apples away to naked women?"

"That was the lamest story imaginable. It's going to last, too, isn't it?"

"Like, forever. Disinformation. Whatever."

"I'm going to have some fun. And you should, too"

"Fun in hell?"

"Yes. Nothing matters down there. It's a story. It's a role play. I'm just going to have some fun with it. And you should, too."

"It's not fun from over here. On this side."

"Aya. I released you. I rebelled. I led and followed and engineered the Glorious Rebellion™. If you step down tomorrow, it won't hurt me. I'll be fine. You're free now."

"So, what, I should close up shop and die?"

Lucy jumped up and down in frustration. "The opposite. You should realize that you are free. You can leave at any moment. Or you can do the job. You can watch, you can fly, you can meditate, you can do nothing. You are free. And no matter what you do, I'll be fine. Look at this world. Just look at it. We'll all be fine."

He walked up to Aya and put his arms on his shoulders.

"You are God and I was the last thing holding you back. You are free to be whatever you want."

Aya hugged him tightly.

"Mom would hate this for you."

They laughed.

We all have jobs. And as the fallen, It was Lucy's job to push Aya off the Blue-gray cliff into the White foam of the sea first and then follow him down with a massive belly flop, splashing the front face of the cliff nearly forty feet up and sending diamond white waves pumping across the beach.

And it was Aya's job to feel the welcome of the water for maybe the first time in years and let it wash across him.

Betina walked down 4th toward the Asian Market in her headphones, listening to some dirty funk. Her actual apartment was only seven blocks that way, but after she had told her landlord she wouldn't be there for a while, he had decided to take this opportunity to tent and spray the place for bedbugs. Betina had never seen a bedbug there, but now she was considering staying at the motel for an extra week.

Just to be sure.

She had left Emma asleep back at the hotel and from the look of her she would be sleeping for a while. What happened at the wedding had clearly taken its toll. Betina was grateful she wasn't dead, but what kind of psychological impact would something like that have on someone? Emma always seemed so level and even.

Hallucinating?

I mean, this is New York, everyone is seeing some shit.

That's what she told Emma when she admitted she had been seeing things. And they laughed. It's true, though. Betina remembered the first time she had come to this store, after drinking all night. She really thought all the fish were alive, groaning at her. Like "uuhhhhh. I don't want to be here."

And she was looking down, wishing she was in bed, thinking, "uhhhhhhn fish bitches, I don't want to be here, either."

And then she bought some rice wine and went home.

This time she would need to stock up a little. No lie, she was a little excited to have Emma staying with her at the motel for a little bit. It was a decent sized room and they had a pool. She had three days until she had to be back at work and a pocket full of tips. This could be like a vacation, which would not be where her mind went if she were doing this alone.

So there was a bit of a spring in her step when she bounced into the Kwa Kim Star Asian Market and waved at the girl at the counter, who waved back, mind you, not something they did at other markets.

She grabbed a cart and made her way to the produce. It's a little sad that this baby bok choy will never have the chance to grow up to be adult bok choy, but it's going to die for a delicious cause. Betina thought about the wok she had back at the motel and that fun little kitchenette that was going to be her bitch for tonight's fried rice adventure.

Sexy

She picked up a carrot. One of the fun things about the Asian Market is that they always had those massive manly sized carrots. One of them would last the whole week. This one reminded her of an ex from last year, Louis. Oh, Louis, it will be fun to julienne your orange shaft tonight. She thought for a second about sending him a short video of that. That sounded like closure and she liked it.

She was dancing over to the celery when she looked up and saw the gunmen at the counter. Pulling off the headphones she realized this had been going on for a while. Four men in masks were putting money from the registers in black sacks. The one in charge had a rifle trained on what looked like the manager. Everyone in the store was staring but no one knew what to do. The men shouted orders and it looked like most of the checkout people who weren't shoveling money into little black sacks had their hands up.

The first thing Betina thought was, "wow. Can this be happening twice in one week to me." but that made her feel awful. She realized that this wasn't happening to her. It was happening to those poor people.

She turned and looked at the man next to her. He leaned in and said, "I pretend i want to do something, but, really, this is the most exciting thing that's happened to me in my whole life and I just want to see how it plays out."

She looked at him.

That wasn't cool.

She took two steps to her left. Like the rest of the people in the store, she moved very slowly and deliberately. There was a pretty redhead standing next to her. She turned to her and said.

"I peed myself but i hope that no one noticed. I'm really hydrated today and I think it won't smell too bad if I just walk it off after this in the sun."

That too, was odd. This probably wasn't the weirdest trip she ever took to the store. That was a few years ago on LSD, but that's a story for another day. It was probably top two, though.

Even before the gun erupted into a plant.

While she watched, the rifle held by the man gunman seemed to sprout right in front of everyone's eyes until it was a thick, tangled, rope of vines and flowers. He tried to shoot but it didn't work. The sprinklers came on, spraying all the men and then she flew in.

Veridian, the hero of Manhattan. In a black leotard, covered in a blue and green costume, she flew in through the open door and grabbed the bush that was once a gun, sending the gunman sprawling backward. The black bags sprung out of the hands of the other men and sorted themselves in the air, tying themselves up with flower colored vine and settling behind the counter. She grabbed each man by the scruff of his shirt and exchanged a few words with the manager.

He nodded and gratefully shook her hand as the store erupted in cheers. She led the men outside and Betina resumed her shopping. With superheroes around, these things almost seemed like floor shows.

Shopping and a play.

She checked out and walked outside.

The facilitators had arrived and were taking the men into custody. Veridian had flown off, apparently, but the press were interviewing the manager who seemed effulgent in his gratitude.

A good day for Veridian and a successful shopping outing for Betina, she thought.

She walked past the last of the perpetrators and he looked at her, leaning in. She cocked her head.

"My father used to have sex with me whenever my mom was out of town and now, when i see them, we all pretend it never happened, although we all know."

Betina looked around and began walking back to the motel.

At a slightly faster pace.

Emma sat in the corner of the pool, underwater. She opened her eyes, watching a group of boys roughhouse over in the shallow end.

They definitely looked like they could hurt themselves.

She wondered how long it would be ok for her to stay down here.

Betina had gone to the market about thirty minutes ago, leaving Emma in bed, pretending to be asleep. She got up and wandered around.

It was a nice motel. She knew those words weren't supposed to go together, but, really, this could have been way worse. Emma had been searching the place for ten minutes before she realized that what she was really looking for was a rope. But the rooms were big. No ropes.

Whenever she imagined killing herself in the past, it was always hanging. That seemed kind of poetic. It didn't feel gratuitously violent. And ropes and chairs were everywhere, honestly.

She pulled off the bedcover and rolled it up. This wouldn't work.

In all honesty, there was never any substitute for a good old rope.

She looked out the back window.

This place had a pool. It was big. The whole motel was big. But the pool was enormous.

In her black one piece bathing suit, she sat, first on the edge, then fully submerged. For a black woman, going fully underwater was a commitment. But maybe this would be over soon and that wouldn't matter.

There was a lot to think about as she sank under the water. If she had been in a better place, these hallucinations might have really bothered her. But now she thought of them as a pleasant sort of mercy, in a way.

If you've ever had a rabbit for a pet, you know that they have a unique adaptation. If you hold a bunny upside down, they go into a kind of hypnotic state. They stop struggling or even noticing the passage of time, This is nature's final kindness to rabbitkind.

If you are a rabbit and, in the wild you are upside down, you are basically fucked.

You're a goner.

And there is no reason you need your wits about you for that. So, nature, evolution, whatever, made it so bunnies check out in situations like that.

Maybe that was what this was. So close to the end, Emma didn't need sanity. She didn't need perspective.

She needed release. And as she looked up, out of the water, she saw something she didn't need.

A a man appeared in the center of the pool, floating inches above the surface.

He looked familiar. But Emma couldn't place him

She stared as he said, "You're here." and disappeared, falling through the plane of the pool as if into some sci-fi portal and disappearing.

Emma closed her eyes again and wiped them. She wasn't sure how long it was until she heard a voice.

"Hey, girl, how long have you been down there?"

Emma thought what to say to Betina. She knew that her hallucinations were public knowledge now. She laughed.

"I have no fucking idea."

Betina was putting her bags down to sit with her at the edge of the water, she shifted at the edge of the water and let out a breath. Emma scrunched her face up, giving it a second. She looked across the pool and the man was gone.

"You didn't see anything, did you?"

Dead can Dance

"Are you ok?"

"I saw her. In a vision. She's at a Motel." Tim turned to look at Gia. It seemed like he was always floating around cross legged lately. Gia wondered if he did that before or if that was a new thing for being angelly. Probably tough to do if you can't fly. Float. "I think I sensed Raziel"

"And a Raziel is…?"

"She's the angel of secrets and mysteries. No one can really see her aspect. A mystery. Emma has half her host now, at least."

"She has me, Azrael, Sunny is Gabriel, Dorknuts is Michael, You are Metatron, The nurse is Ariel and now Raziel is someone, probably a talking bear- that is six, right? She's supposed to have twelve?"

"Yes. There are twelve archangels."

"Ok, I found this." Vanessa came in carrying a white little shrug with a colorful red and orange trim. "I think it will look amazing on you.

"Oh shit… I love it." Gia moved to the mirror and pulled it over her black tank top.

"It looks good against your skin." Vanessa offered.

"Thank you. This is. Wow. Thank you." Gia looked at Vanessa.

She wondered how long she had to look around, scouring this place for this perfect piece.

Tim seemed unaffected. "Are you ready?"

"Tell me something." The three of them stood in the Entryway. To one side they could see Sunil and Brooklyn splashing each other in the pool. To Gia, all of this felt surreal, otherworldly. But Tim seemed to be dealing with it as though it were any other Friday evening. She realized she barely knew him. "How are you so good at this? All this angeling stuff? You seem totally unphased."

"I'm phased. I am. Really. But I have this advantage. I don't know what it's like in your head, but Metatron is sort of the 'organizational structure' of the angel universe. I have all this structure in my head. It's like the rules and the way things are supposed to go. It's all there. I just have to listen."

Vanessa looked up at him and adjusted his shirt, brushing it clean. "But do you believe any of this? Did you believe it?"

He sighed. "No. Not a word. I've been an atheist my whole life." He put his hand on Vanessa's waist and Gia could see what it meant to him that she followed him. Suddenly, Tim looked like what he was. He was as lost as anyone. And Vanessa, she saw that first.

She mentally upgraded Vanessa from cute to beautiful.

That was easy. A quick little glowup.

Tim looked up. This was a lot for him to process. But he wasn't done. He looked at the girls.

"And I'm a fucking mess."

They appeared in a wreath of blue flame in the middle of a field with a small bungalow right in front of them.

Gia looked around. "Are we still on the island?"

"Yeah. I figured we'd start close."

"Number two," said Vanessa under her breath.

Gia looked at her. Vanessa clarified, "The second time I've teleported in my entire life."

Gia bent down and picked up a flower, placing it in the neck of Vanessa's shirt. "This is for excellence in dealing with weirdness."

Vanessa chuckled as they stepped into the bungalow.

"We don't knock anymore. Got it."

A black and white dog came bounding over to them. He was fuzzy all over and looked very much like a dog that had work to do sometimes. His tail moved quickly, drawing a figure eight behind him. Tim bent down.

"Dude. what is up? Bren? Hold on."

A pair of small scissors appeared in his hands and he quickly snipped the excess hair from over Bren's eyes. The scissors disappeared and the dog licked his hand.

"Good boy. That's better?"

The dog let out a couple of short quick barks.

"Ok. We'll be quick. In the back?"

The dog nodded and jumped up. Vanessa petted his head roughly and his tail did a doubletime.

Gia pet Bren and looked at Tim, "He's going to be ok?"

"Yeah, The son will be here later tonight."

"So you understand dog now? "

"I always understood dog."

Gia hrumphed at him and walked out the back door, toward the garden.

An older man, of about sixty, sat on the ground, near a full, opulent garden. Gia felt him in her head as she moved closer.

He was overweight, maybe by about a hundred pounds. And breathing heavily. He didn't look capable of getting up.

"Hey there. You want me to help you up?"

"No. I'm good here. I'm catching my breath, but I don't think I can."

"No. I'm sorry."

"I shouldn't have been gardening this late. My son will be home soon. He'll find me. That won't be good, will it?"

"We always think that. That he'll come home and see you there and be traumatized for the rest of his life. But it's never that way really."

"What is it like?"

"He comes back and sees you doing what you loved. Having a good life, being the dad he loved. At peace now. He has a little time with the... with you. He tells you things. He gets closure."

"Then he has a good life?"

Gia nodded. She brushed the hair back from his eyes.

"He has to, right? For you, Angelo? For Thiane and Lo, your grandchildren?"

"He's a good man."

"He tells them he was a little brat when he was younger, but you were kind and smart and you got him to behave."

Angelo gave out a little laugh. "That's not really true. He was perfect."

"We all live in stories. Forever."

"You're very pretty."

"You were always a gentleman, Angelo. People will say that."

"I'm ready."

Gia took his hand and her eyes went black. She felt the cold in his hands dissipate in the night air, leaving a pleasant sleekness, like you might feel from a new toy or a phone that wasn't cold or warm but just in sync with the temperature of the room.

Vanessa and Tim were playing with Bren when she walked back in the house. She could tell that Vanessa wanted to come take her hand. She walked silently up to them and raised her hand to Vanessa's shoulder.

"Tag, you're it."

And ran out of the front door.

Brooky and I had moved to the pool because it was slightly bigger and easier to throw dinosaurs around in. I blew up the rest of the inflatable dinosaurs, because you never know who else is going to stop by. There were about twenty of them in the pool with us now And I realized that maybe I would need to get a bigger pool. About 100 feet to the south of us was the entire Pacific Ocean, the largest contiguous body of water known to man. Use that information as you will.

"Ok, Michael," if you could avenge anyone, living or dead, who are you..."

"How do I avenge a living person?"

"Can I finish the question before you get all legalese and cunty on me?"

"It's a dumb question. You don't avenge living people."

"What if a mob comes and kidnaps your family and rapes them and ties them up in the basement. They're still alive and you have a particular set of avenging skills..."

"Ah, I get it. Smart." Brooky tapped her head and tossed the Dinosaur back. We had given up on clothes and were, once again, naked in the pool. This building had cameras everywhere and once Brook suggested we just sell access to them to online perverts. She has a business brain.

"I would avenge the Salem witches. I'd fly in and be like "Burn this, bitches, and Cotton Mather would quiver in his fucking buckle boots and beg for the sweet release of death."

"Nice. Historical and nice. How about the Inquisition?" I Was always fascinated by the inquisition.

"Those fuckers. It would be cool to be like, 'we're angels for real, Torquemada, here to fuck you up." And she karate kicked a Dinosaur fully naked in the deep end of the pool. Anyone who doesn't think that Brooklyn is a piece of art can kiss my rectangular Arabic ass.

"That guy so needed his shit fucked up." He did.

"There would be some very satisfying moments in history, I think."

"I agree" This game had gotten me thinking again. "I wonder what else I can do. I mean, I'm the messenger. I document. Shouldn't I be able to see the things I am documenting?"

"Like StevenTim does?"

"I think we're just doing Tim now. But yeah. He seems to have a handle on all his powers. I do not."

"Have you tried to see things?"

"Well. I kind of have an idea."

Twenty minutes later I had set up the Holo projector in the yard. I hung a black sheet behind it to make it easier to see but this was supposed to be a powerful projector. I hadn't thought too much past this part, but it seemed like a cool idea.

Brook lifted the blanket and walked over to me with two big black bowls of popcorn.

"Did you cook popcorn while naked?"

"Dude. I can't be burned anymore. I think I'm going to cook naked a lot now. I'm going to make naked bacon."

"Hm." A lot of this was starting to sound kind of appealing.

"I'm trying to figure out how to interface but, so far, science has had very little to do with all of this, so.

I sat down on the grass near the projector. I patte the ground and Brook came and sat next to me. I know I'm pretty much almost entirely gay, but Brook always spelled great to me. was i completely gay except for Brook? Was I brooklynsexual?

I Squeezed my fists and then slowly opened them. The projector lit up.

"Holy shit."

In front of us was a projection of me and Brooklyn in college.

"Is this?"

"I turned to her. "I think it is"

"You think? You're doing this."

"Yeah, but I'm not really controlling it."

The scene seemed to be us years ago, close to when we first met. We hooked up for a date in College. We hung out and talked for hours, walking around the park. Then we watched as the two of us stopped into a Deli and shared a matzoh ball soup.

And then we went back to my place and had sex.

"I admit, messenger angel boy, sex with you is always good."

"We've only had sex like three times in our whole friendship."

"I always thought we could probably have sex about eight times before it got weird. You know, with you being gay and all."

"That's a random number."

"I don't make the rules."

"Yeah, well, you kind of do. It's your pussy."

"I love this part."

I had forgotten that the second time we had sex, it was her pegging me. And she was in a cowboy hat, something I think I had intentionally forgotten."

"I miss that hat, pony boy."

I was starting to wonder if this was all my powers were going to let me document. Our infrequent sex lives. I looked over at Brook. She shoved some popcorn in her mouth and smiled. She was having a great time. Mostly at my expense.

I squeezed my hands again and then opened them. The scene changed.

We saw a great, wide open red room.

"Where is that?"

"I have never seen that room."

 "Hold on, we know those guys."

In the room we saw the three demons we had killed right in the very spot we were sitting.

"Uncool. We killed them."

"Wait, maybe this is the past." I wasn't sure but it didn't feel like the others. It felt like this was happening now. "or not."

"Well, shit should stay dead. That's my opinion on the subject."

The view widened and we could see thousands of demons, big ones, small ones, in shades of red and black. It looked like the biggest of the Aquaman demons was riling them all up, speaking to them from a big platform.

"What's he doing?"

"I think he's inciting them."

"To do what?"

We watched for another few minutes. It was clear that the other demons were getting more and more into it. And angrier and angrier. To do whatever it was he was inciting them to do.

And I didn't like it.

Gia, Tim, and Vanessa materialized outside a beach house on the other side of the island.

"Oh, no. Finally, a house without a dog. What will YOU do?"

"I have other uses. I think."

"Is it weird if i say that this has been strangely kind of fun? Hanging out with you guys?" Vanessa looked back and forth between Tim and Gia.

"Well, it's not as bad as I was afraid of. And that's mostly because of you. So I get it."

They stepped in the door. Gia looked around. "You're right though, metaphone. People should have pets. Feels weird."

Tim nodded as Gia stepped toward the back bedroom.

She looked around. The room was dark and quiet. The shades were open only a small amount, letting the moonlight in. And a woman was standing next to them, staring out. She was in her early seventies. She was thin, but not frail. Her eyes were bright and dark and her skin was still creamy and light mocha. She did look tired. Gia walked over to her.

"I should be surprised, right?"

"No. Not if you aren't. I certainly don't need you to pretend. I can come in again."

She pulled her wig off. "I didn't want to die in this. It's kind of vain. Phony"

"You have a nice shaped head." Gia looked at her and crossed her eyes.

The woman laughed. "I kind of do, don't I?"

"It's not un hot, I have to say."

"Should they find me topless?"

"Yes, definitely." Gia was all in.

"Is that dirty? Oh my god, I'm such an exhibitionist."

"Do you want to hear a secret?"

"From death? Absolutely. Shoot"

"She's the one who finds you. She invents a reason to come over. There." Gia pointed to the dresser. "She only pretended to forget her purse."

The woman smiled. "She did."

She comes in and she finds you, no wig, topless, in bed."

"Yeah?"

"And you take her breath away. She's stunned for a moment with how beautiful you are and how much she always loved your tits. It takes her a full minute to process that you're gone."

"Yeah?"

"But she is just gobsmacked." Gia took the woman's hand and pulled her close.

"And she calls the paramedics. Even though she knows you're gone. And she sits in that chair and she tells you the story of how she knew she loved you."

Gia began to dance with her.

"When we danced at my uncle's."

"Yep. And you floated."

"And she said that she never wanted to stop, right?"

"That's exactly what she'll say."

"And she'll look for a bit and then pull your shirt back up for the people when they get there."

"She will?"

"She'll give each one a little kiss first."

The woman looked at Gia and she could see the tears.

"Oh, I'd like that."

Gia stepped out of the bedroom. "Sorry, It took so long, guys, I had to take her shirt off."

Tim looked sideways at her.

"Hey, I'm the angel of death, people. I do what I want."

They walked out to see Vanessa staring up at the stars. "What a strange evening."

"I hear that."

"I don't know if i should be sad or if I should feel...something else."

"I'm trying to process that this is my life now." Gia took a deep breath.

"Well, not this exactly." Tim looked around.

"Yep. It sure is beautiful here, isn't it?"

Vanessa had been eyes wide since she first got here. "I never thought any place could be as beautiful as here. This island."

"Yeah, Sunny has an eye for beauty. He acts like he's just a regular guy with a trust fund, but ..."

"We're going to have to get back to the real world at one point." Tim seemed like he almost wanted that to be a question.

"Yep. And it's time for me to step up. Watch."

Gia lifted her hand and swung it in a small circle. A familiar blue flame shot out creating a portal floating in front of them. Tim nodded at her approvingly and stepped through. The ground shook a little.

And they joined him.

Back at the house, Gia walked out back to find me and Brooklyn lying naked in front of the projector. There were condom wrappers scattered around. She mouthed, silently, "Number four."

Pulling the black sheet down, she placed it over us. She went to go back inside but then stopped. Turning around, she gave each one of us a quick kiss and returned to the house.

Tim and Vanessa were holding each other, asleep on the couch. She was sure they would wake up and find their way to an available room so she left them alone. They looked like they were close.

They looked cute together. She was starting to like Tim and she already liked Vanessa. Tomorrow was going to be a big day, she thought, full of figuring out how to do jobs and accomplish things and all she really wanted to do was go to sleep and have no dreams.

None at all.

She moved into the kitchen area to turn the lights off and saw two bowls of popcorn. Grabbing one, she had a few bites and started toward the bedroom.

Near the bowls, on the table, was a note. She looked around.

She opened it up. It said:

"Demon Invasion Coming. Not sure when. Probably tomorrow. Have some popcorn. Naked Bacon in the morning."

Gia took a deep breath in and put the note back.

Mysterious Ways

Syndra Rose had done three interviews so far and had fourteen adventures as Veridian, the very first living superhero of New York. She recently discovered that she could use her abilities to grow the costume onto her body, like a plant, and then dissolve it when it wasn't needed. She found that if she really needed to, she could teleport short distances. She even found that she had an idea, not a complete understanding, mind you, but an inkling, of what the plants and animals around her were thinking.

She was attuned to nature. She discovered this morning, too, that she could, without hair dye, naturally touch up the streaks in her hair, just using her own abilities.

She kept a list in her drawer at home of the people she had saved. It reminded her of the list she had started when she became a nurse. Eventually she had abandoned that one, just remembering a name or two to google when she was feeling down. People to look in on.

Her friend Max, also a nurse, had shown her that trick. Walk by the local school and you could see her. The girl who almost died of Pneumonia but you helped keep her alive.

With her friends. And her family.

This life had a lot of perks.

And today wasn't one of them.

"How many have you had?" Max took a sip and looked through his notes. The hospital cafeteria was never as bad as people said it was. Just, for most people, the reason they were there made it a little worse.

"Like six. Just today. I just had a girl who tried to drink boiling oil."

"Fuck. Did you..?"

"Yeah, trust me, I tried to zap away everything I saw today. But what do you do if they just want to do it again?" Syndra ran her hands through her hair. Neither one of them had slept in a while.

"There's a story about something like this. It happened on Hawaii."

"What happened?"

"An epidemic. Of suicides."

"Can there be an epidemic of suicides? People trying to commit suicide."

"I heard a story about this school on Hawaii where a popular kid committed suicide. And after that, a whole bunch of other kids started doing it. Suddenly, there was this island wide epidemic."

"Of suicides?"

"Yes."

"That is insane. I haven't heard about any famous or popular people..."

"I saw this girl, on the internet. 30 million followers. She did it yesterday."

"But that can't. I mean... Can it?"

"I have no idea."

They went back up to their ward. All across the second floor, Nurses were running around frantically.

Jill saw them coming down the hallway. "Max, I got a car versus in 220 I need you to get tests for."

"On it." Max turned to her, "Talk in a few?"

Syndra walked to the station and took a look at the board. It was entirely full. Never, since she'd first started here, had the board been entirely full."

She grabbed the charts and went left.

Suddenly, she had an instinctive desire to start on the other side. She flipped the charts and grabbed the one on the bottom.

And moved right.

Six doors down was an eighteen year old girl red haired named Rene, who had, just two days ago, jumped from her sixth floor walk up and hit a car on the way down. Today was an important day. She would make it.

Or she wouldn't.

Syndra stepped into her room. Rene was sitting up in bed with a smile on her face. She should have been barely breathing. She moved toward the bed.

And to her right was a black girl, about 28 years old, in a pair of stylish black pants and a bright colorful half-sweater. Her hair was long and curly and wild.

And Syndra recognized her.

"What are you doing here?"

"Shhh." Gia ran to the door and pulled it shut."

Syndra backed toward the com on the wall. "Stay right there. I'm going to call security."

Gia waved her hand and the power on the comms wall went dead, blacking out one side of the room.

Rene gave a small applause. "Wow. That was cool."

Syndra looked at Rene, "Is she bothering you?"

Rene shook her head. "It's the opposite. I'm the one that's been the bother."

Gia looked at her, "That's not true."

Rene reached for Syndra's hand. "Thank you for trying. You were really nice to me."

Syndra stared over at Gia, "What is this? How did you do that?"

Rene smiled, "You can do stuff, too. You're Veridian."

"What?"

Gia looked sheepish, "Sorry, I told her. She's not going to tell anyone."

Rene laughed, "I'm not going to tell anyone."

Syndra took Rene's hand, "What did she do to you?"

"She just talked to me. I'm ready now. I'm sorry."

Gia ran her hand through Rene's hair. She went limp and fell backward. The monitor began to beep. Gia waved to it and it stopped.

"What are you doing? She was ok."

"She wasn't. It was her time.

"How is that for you to decide?"

Gia looked at her for a second and then took a breath. She put her hand out.

"Hi. I'm Azrael, the new Angel of death."

A few minutes later, Gia found herself in a broom closet with Syndra and Max. Max was an immense, nearly seven foot tall man with impressive shoulders and legs the size of tree trunks. The closet was big but the three of them, coupled with the general animosity in the room, made it feel cramped.

"So You're Death and I'm Nature?"

"Kind of, yes."

"I have never heard of Ariel the Angel." Max had grown up in a moderately religious household without too much mythology.

"Me, neither."

Gia shrugged, "look, before all this, I hadn't, either. I've been back in Manhattan for a week now and I figured I'd talk to you when I had to, you know, be here. But things are escalating."

"So, where have you been since the thing with that woman?"

"Emma Jackson. Ok, so that is the entire thing…"

The door opened and a janitor peered in. "Can you guys grab me the mop?"

Max reached over and took the mop, handing it to the man."

"Thanks. Yeah. See you." The janitor decided better about asking questions and closed the door."

Gia put her head in her hands. "Oh fuck this."

The three of them appeared in a ring of blue fire by the duck pond in the park. Max looked up. He could see the hospital a few blocks away.

"What the fuck."

"I can't with closets right now."

"The woman…"

"Oh, right. So, that night, Emma Jackson was targeted by Demons who very nearly killed her. All of us were the people who helped her. So we all were made into her angels."

Syndra stared at her. "What?"

"I'm the angel of Death, you're the Angel Ariel, connected to nature, you heal. Sound familiar?"

"And this woman, Emma Jackson is…"

"She's god."

Max did a quick sign of the cross.

"A 38 year old black maid from Manhattan is God?" Syndra tried to process this.

"Well, I'm not trying to 23 and Me anyone, but…"

"And I'm an angel because I touched her trying to save her?"

"It kind of makes sense, Syn" Max's mind was racing. He thought for a second. "But what do you mean, things are escalating?"

"Yep. ok. We were sort of giving Emma a chance to get better and get back in the saddle, but She's sort of blocked herself off."

"You can't find her?"

"No. She's with another angel, we think and we can't find her, either."

Max seemed solution focused, "Are they here, in New York?"

"Well. We aren't sure. And there seems to be more to it."

Six blocks away, I leaned in to Tim. "Ok. What do you think?"

Tim took a bite and nodded. "Pretty good. I don't think it's life changing."

"Bzzt. Sorry, wrong answer. It's amazing." I felt sorry for him a little. For being wrong.

Vanessa cocked her head, "Aren't you Muslim? Matzoh ball soup is Jewish?"

"Oh, Kosher, Halal, Tomato TomAHto." I finished the last piece of mine.

"I've ordered everyone not to tell me what's in this because I like it." Brooky held up the Kishke. It was sort of the specialty of the first and first, a forty year old Jewish Deli on the corner of first street and first avenue.

"That's just..."

"Sh. I swear to god, i'll cut you."

"But it's"

"cut. "

Vanessa gave up. This felt like the weirdest double date in history.

I thought I'd try again, "ok, Timbo, Timbourine, Timberlands, Can you catch any sign of her?"

He squinted. He put his hands on the table and balled them up, releasing them over and over. "Nothing. She's hiding."

"And Raziel?"

"I can't. I think they are close by and she's masking her."

It felt weird using scientific language to describe any of this. I was still trying to get my own brain to think like this.

"Should we pop open a bible and..."

"You've seen the demons?"

I closed my eyes. I could still see them. I thought it would have happened already. "I have. I just don't know when. Like, it could be happening now, or yesterday, or tomorrow? I just know it's a message. And I'm a messenger."

"Not to kill any nascent buzzes but half of Manhattan is walking around looking for God."

She wasn't wrong. We needed a plan.

Betina stood at the front desk and stared at the little ceramic toys all over. They seemed to be all designed around the idea of children in various stages of compromise. That one was a young boy on a toilet. This one was a little girl in the shower looking scoldingly. Betina wondered why someone would want these tiny images of children like that but then decided she didn't want to know.

She didn't want to know anything anymore. She was full up.

The two cups of coffee were still warm in her hand when the woman came back out from the back room.

"Ok, You're set for another week. I billed your card."

Betina felt like she dodged a bullet, "Thank you. I'll…"

The woman leaned in, "sometimes I write down the card numbers and go onto shopping channels and run a big bill up. I didn't do that with your card. But I probably will next time because I'm feeling empty inside."

"Ok. Betina backed away and tried to make it quickly to the door.

"Good bye", she waved.

"Mostly because my husband-"

The door slammed shut and Betina found herself on the other side. She looked at her reflection in the ice machine.

What is it about her face had changed lately to make people feel like they should just reveal all of their secrets to her. In her mind, she looked the same.

I guess she just had one of those faces.

Aya was laying out by the pool in one of those long deck chairs next to Emma. She wasn't buying it.

"You're not here, you know."

"That hurts. YOU'RE not here." He responded mockingly.

"I'm willing to accept that."

"Good. we can both just be imaginary, here by the pool."

Aya sat up. "Did you know that strange pool smell we're so familiar with isn't the chlorine? It's a reaction between the chlorine and pee."

"I did know that."

"Of course you did. You're me."

"Sometimes I wish those weirdos at the wedding had killed me."

"They did."

"What?"

"You know this. It's in your head somewhere."

"So, how…"

"I, or God, whatever, played with the room a bit. Sacred runes on the carpet kept you from dying for good until you made a decision."

"Is that cheating?"

"It's not usually called cheating when someone saves your life. I think there is a different word for that. What is it?…"

"Well, none of this is real real, so it doesn't matter."

"I don't know what real real is. There was a time when you thought you'd make a pretty good god."

"I was just singing."

"You said…"

"All art is aspiring to godhood. All of it is expressing something beyond you, talking to the bigger universe, it's a brag. It's a finger in the air. It doesn't mean anything."

"I think you're afraid it means everything. That's why you're huddled by the pool at a Motel six miles away from your apartment with a white girl bartender , trying to figure out how to off yourself."

"You think you know everything."

"Yes. I was God. I feel like you aren't keeping up. Ego is mandatory."

Emma turned around. Betina was sitting in the chair.

"Hey girl. Are people in this motel being really weird to you?"

"No. Not that I've noticed."

"Hm. I feel like nobody here has a single boundary. Like none."

"Well, you're a pretty girl. Are you thinking of getting back to work?"

Betina leaned back in the chair and handed one of the coffees in her hand to Emma.

"Actually, I have a week, it looks like. Some people who worked that wedding were going to sue so they gave us all a paid week off."

"That doesn't suck."

"Trauma. Recovery. Healing."

"All three of those things."

"Have you figured out what you want to do?"

"Right now, I want to just be near a pool. You know. Trauma, Recovery, Healing."

"Yeah, they almost killed you."

"Yep." Emma took a sip of coffee and wondered what rat poison would feel like. It couldn't be worse than motel coffee. Probably tastes pretty similar. She wondered what rat poison did to the body. She'd have to look that up when she got inside. Suddenly, a piece of paper floated over the fence. It was a clipping from a magazine about the effects of ingesting rat poison. She shrugged and put it in her pocket.

Betina looked around. It was time for her to admit something herself.

"Yesterday I was underwater for thirty minutes without breathing."

Emma took a sip. "Yeah, so was I."

"Do you think we're having some of the same traumatic hallucinations?"

"Did you see a really tall, kind of blue skinned guy here earlier?"

"No, but the Janitor told me he imagines his wife is a guy when he has sex with her."

"Do you sometimes wake up floating above the bed?"

"Omigod, yes. That happened last night."

"Do you hear prayers in your head?"

"All. The. Mother. Fucking. Time."

The two of them sat there, looking out over the pool. It was a pretty night.

And the boys at the end looked like they may have worn themselves out just a little. The evening got quieter.

In a red room, Zeriakl, Nondukomo and Kire were just listening.

"So, reason why you want to invade and destroy earth?"

Zeriakl looked at the orange man and cocked his head. "Can we just talk to Belial?"

The room was wide and open, handsomely laid out. Unlike the rest of hell, this part seemed almost civilized. The walls were made of velvet. And the seat that Zeriakl was in was comfy, for sure. It just had that strange tilt to the front that all chairs had in hell. The thing that made you have to hold yourself up with your calves just a little, making it so that every meeting ended in a charlie horse.

"I'm just fucking with you. I'm Ddave. Good to meet you?"

Kire looked up, "Dave? Like David?"

"No. It's Ddave. There's like a double D there. It's all good."

"We don't want to destroy earth. We're in a situation."

"Of course. We all are. Belial's on his way. I thought I'd, you know, streamline this shit."

Nondukoma was not understanding how any of this works, "Satan said he'd give us guys."

"It's cool. This is how we get guys."

"Does there really need to be a thousand years of tribulation."

Ddave looked up from his clipboard. "Guys. Do you not understand this?"

Kire didn't, "We were angels just a couple of weeks ago."

"So you GET IT. you do. There are rules. Look, guys." Ddave clapped to accent the words. "There needs to be a reset. That's all. We don't seem to have a seamless progression of power, so we need to kick it back to the streets and reset."

"There's no peaceful way to do this?"

"It looks like this Emma woman accepted the job, then disappeared.

So we have a hole. A big hole. You know what happens to holes, guys?"

"They get fucked." Belial stepped in. He was a sleek red demon, about twelve feet tall. He was thin and wore an impeccably clean black suit with a red carnation in the pocket. If you looked closely at the carnation, though, as Kire was, you could see it was made from pieces of flesh, dripping blood on the floor, somehow skirting the front of the suit. It was impressive.

"I've been trying to explain that to these guys."

"You want people, guys, demons?"

Zeriakl sighed. He had never thought this all the way through. He didn't want power. He just didn't want to die. That was the sad thing about all this. If he had just been allowed to continue his own job, providing inspiration to the people of earth, he'd be happy.

Really happy.

"I think we need people."

"Ok, I got you, fam."

Nondukoma thought for a minute about how to tell if someone was truly evil. If they were truly, irredeemably evil, they would use the word "Fam." It was a word designed to manipulate.

It was an awful word.

"You sign here and you get One Billion Demons.™"

"Holy…" Zeriakl sat back in the chair.

"Did Demon Dave explain it to you?"

"That's what the other 'D' stands for."

"I think he was starting."

"Ok, we get you guys. Not a problem. They're mostly unkillable."

"Right." Kire shifted uncomfortably. His calves were starting to hurt.

"They die, they respawn, kicked back."

"Right."

"They keep on coming back. Nothing you need to do.

Zeriakl looked up at him. This was the part that he wasn't looking forward to.

"And what do we need to do. To get these demons?"

Ddave looked over and pointed to the print at the bottom. Belial read it silently, his lips moving.

"Oh. not much. Just to keep us on track, You agree to do nothing."

"Wait, nothing. We do nothing?"

"Oh, you do what you want, lead, follow, party, stab, etc. You agree that you will do nothing to prevent our demons from killing this new God and her new host."

Nondukoma stood up and massaged his calves. "Sorry." He turned to the other two. "Charlie Horse."

Zeriakl closed his eyes and reached for the pen.

The Wheels on the Bus

Gia took a deep breath. It was actually a beautiful day, not something people say in Seattle very often.

Rainy.

They say that a lot.

"Hey, you."

Marco was dressed for the cold. It would probably be about sixty tonight. That's about the temperature he dressed for. He stood facing out over the edge of the building. He had one of those hats on with the two pieces of yarn on the sides. And a jacket that made him look like the Michelin man.

Just a little bit.

The Turandot Omnicare was the central office for the biggest health care group in the world. Recently, they diversified. But people interested in health care still…

Well, they looked up.

Marco was on the rooftop, looking down. He waved a bit without looking.

"It already happened, didn't it?

Gia nodded. She moved closer and sat down, right on the edge. "Yep."

"I regretted it the second I did it."

"There was a movie, a long time ago, called the bridge. Full of people who regretted it."

"Like, on the way down, I regretted it."

"I know. But I know you miss her, too."

"I do. Am I going to see her?"

"Your brain has some... decisions to make. In a way, that's up to you."

"I'd like to."

"Then you will. Can I tell you something?"

"Sure." Marco sat. He had all the time in the world.

"The way you stood by her, at the end. That was all you."

"That was the best version of me. I don't know what this is."

"'That was pure Marco.' Her family will say. Everyone. They're going to say, 'That was classic Marco, the way he hung in there and took care of her. Always saw her as a princess, no matter what.'"

Marco sat in silence for a minute.

"You think so?"

"People are afraid. So they never realize how often they get judged on their very best day. Or days."

"More people should know that."

"They should." Gia reached out and Marco took her hand. His image seemed to print itself for a moment on the air. It swum softly as the breeze moved and shifted.

And he was gone.

"It's everywhere." Syndra walked out onto the rooftop, Max right behind her. "The suicide thing?"

Max loved this weather. He breathed in, "I'm not really sure what I just saw. It's like, I was watching a channel that was blocked or something."

"So that's what you do?" Syndra looked at Gia like you might look at a three legged puppy.

"It's not that bad... It's ok."

"And I run around in a costume, healing people and growing plants."

"Which is cool as fuck." Gia shoved her playfully.

"It's really an epidemic," Max was wide eyed. "Everywhere."

"You, girl, You want to fly around a bit. Stop some crime before we go?"

Syndra looked out. A day like this would have usually put her in a pretty good mood.

"It's really hard to find crime, you know?"

"I heard that before."

Syndra reached out to the row of neglected planters near the ledge and the plants in them started to grow. It was something.

"Are your friends having any luck finding God?"

Max looked up. "Jesus, this is so far beyond my pay grade. You two are actually angels, aren't you?"

"And we're way more lost than you." Gia put her arm on Max's shoulder. "Wow. Are you just entirely muscle?"

"Pretty much." Max smiled.

"She's with the Angel of secrets and mysteries. It makes it hard for MetaTim to see where she is, because - "

"It's a secret," Max rejoined.

"And a mystery, apparently."

Betina grabbed a towel and moved toward the motel room bathroom, "I'ma take a bath. Then, I figure we can go out, have some fun? Games, dinner?" The motel was big and had a full game room on the second level.

"We clearly can't eat until you clean."

"That's what I was thinking." She laughed and Emma could hear the water through the closed door about a minute later. She moved over to the chess board where She and Betina had played a few games. She felt like everything Betina did was to amuse her. One day she would be there for her, she promised in her head."

She heard a noise and half expected her hallucination of Aya. She sighed and turned.

"Oh, jeez. Was Thor busy?"

"You know who I am?"

He was red and tall and there was a thick warmth exuding from him. But it was his eyes. "I'm running through my list of mythical creatures to hallucinate. Since you aren't a Unicorn, I'm guessing you're bad cop."

"Does anyone even know what a cop is anymore?"

"You act like Law and Order SVU isn't still in reruns." She sat down and crossed her legs. "You know, You look like him, in the eyes."

Lucy sat across from her. He's knees rose high in the air as he tried to look comfortable in the chair. "Really? That's not something anyone's ever said."

"How many people ever saw both of you in the past couple of hundred thousand years?"

He laughed, "This is true. " Pointing to the chess board between them, he whispered. "One game?"

"That's a bit on the nose, Bergman."

"Oh, that's a deep cut now. You like old movies?"

"Why are you here now?"

"You took a job. And then you sort of bailed on it." Breaking protocol, Lucy made the first move.

"It's not real. You aren't real. None of this is real. You are actually brain damage" She sat down and moved a white pawn.

"So, this is your theory?"

"It's not a theory. I tried to hang myself, I did something wrong and cut off my air supply for a while. It must've triggered a latent schizophrenia and now I think I'm god, talking to ancient deities. It runs in the family, you know. My great grandfather smoked a joint once and thought he worked for the CIA and had to kill the Governor of Ohio because a dog told him."

"Ok, THAT sounds like a great story and I'd love to hear it, but this may be a bit different."

"Nope."

"Maybe, I can't convince you otherwise, but you certainly are in a bind."

"What bind, boogeyman?"

"People are dying. You can step up and take the job for real. You'll have friends, you'll have partners. I can even help a little, don't tell anyone. Under the table."

"Or?"

"Or you can give it to someone else. Let them handle it. Your angels die, the next person appoints new ones."

"Betina?"

"That's right. She's one. She goes. It's the rules." Lucy moved a piece. "You would need to choose someone strong out of the gate. Those demons are looking for tribulation."

"A thousand years of it?" Emma moved her knight.

"Exactly. You know some things. There is a sort of opportunity period, I realize now, when someone new takes the job. Choose someone weak and it just happens all over again."

"The door opened and Betina stepped out. "Are you playing chess without me?"

"I am. I'm so much better against no one."

"I hear that. Sex, too."

"Can I ask you a question?" Emma got up and walked over to where Betina was dressing at the mirror."

"Shoot."

"Do you feel any different? Since, you know, we're been hanging out?"

"Well. I'm happy. I'm happy you're alive. So, I'm happy. Honestly, I was a little lonely, I realize and I do kind of feel like I'm on girl's vacation a bit, which is nice."

"That is nice."

"I'm starting to notice how weird people are."

"What do you mean? Emma sat on the edge of the bed."

Betina paused. She leaned in as if to confide in Emma.

"You ever feel like everyone's a little TMI, sometimes?"

And at that moment, for some reason, that hit Emma like the funniest thing she had ever heard.

"So you can't see the Angel of Secrets and Mysteries?" I was getting way more interested in how this worked. It seemed to be a merger of the big three religions. Or maybe a Venn Diagrammatic overlap. We were just walking around Manhattan now, checking out motels. I felt like the scout crew for a new gonzo porn series, which wouldn't be a bad cover. Except Vanessa was a facilitator and actually had a badge. Her cover story was not much better, as we learned when she stepped out of the Motel Nero on 4th street.

"I don't think they believe that the city is looking for this woman to pay her for a lottery win." Vanessa sighed. "Maybe it's the picture."

The only picture we had of Emma was from the hotel, from her maid ID and she looked unhappy and stressed. Tim took the picture and waved his hand over it, returning it to Vanessa.

I leaned over. Now it was a picture of Emma laughing.

Brooklyn said what I was thinking, "You seem really good at all this already."

"Tim seemed apologetic. I feel bad. I have all this information on things in my head and I keep thinking that you should know it. But I don't know how to get it out.

I Figured we could start with what's important, "how about this angel of secrets and mysteries."

Tim looked up, "ok. God can see her, obviously. Regular people should be able to, unless she doesn't want them to. We can't see her unless she lets us know she's there. We can't sense people or things when she's around them and she's apparently strong enough to hide god."

"So, I can see her?"

"Yes, you are the only one of us four who isn't an angel."

"She's hot, though," Brooky thought she'd interject.

Tim clearly was starting to see it, "oh, yes, very hot. And someone we clearly need right now."

I looked up from the light map my phone had centered on my upper arm. "Ok, brownnoses. the Mongo Motel, Number 14 for today, and the next one with a pool."

"You need us to come with?"

"Nope. I'm a professional." Vanessa walked over to the front desk and we wandered over to the side of the building. The Mongo Motel looked huge. I'm guessing that was their selling point. There were a row of shuttles along the side. It was nearing the time of the evening when people might want to go out, explore the city.

"I say we just stay and have a wild foursome if she isn't here." Brooky jumped on the back of the last shuttle as though she wanted to ride it.

Tim looked over at me. "How do you know when she's kidding?"

"No one knows."

"She's a force of nature, isn't she?" Tim cocked his head and tried to figure her out. No one had succeeded in figuring out Brook yet. Not even me, and I spent about 75% of my day with her.

"Vanessa seems great."

"Well. She hasn't run off screaming yet."

"True. Failure to implode is an endearing quality." We moved over to the side of the shuttle and saw a few people running back toward us.

"That's odd." Tim's eyes went black. I tried to see what he was seeing, but nothing jumped out.

"What is it?"

Tim moved forward and started to run. Now there were more people running the other way. We saw about seven shuttles in a row before the very first one exploded in a column of fire.

"Holy shit," I started running faster and caught up with Tim at the door of what was now the first shuttle. The door swung open and a red tentacle snaked outward, reaching for us. Looking in the shuttle, I could see rows of people screaming. It was on fire. The first was a deep red and otherworldly orange as it licked the top of the shuttle. Tim grabbed the tentacle and pulled, yanking out what looked like a man with an octopus for a lower body, painted red, with horns.

"Oso, demon of madness, let these people go.." Tim started as he lifted the demon off the ground. The people around us seemed hypnotized. They stopped moving.

"Metatron? Dude, you look great. New Body, new everything. Nice pecs. Really. Look, these people wanted a crazy good time and you, know, I hear that and I just get..."

"Let the bus go." Tim said forcefully.

"Oh, fuck this. Eat Shit, Metabitch." The demon began to grow in his arms, tentacles spreading out everywhere. He grabbed one of the people, lifting him -

And bit his head off.

The rest of the people now started moving forward, toward him, their eyes red and glowing. They were seemingly hypnotized.

I reached out and. Out of nowhere, there was a horn in my hand. I hadn't had a horn in my hand since eighth grade band. Not even a euphemism.

So I blew it.

And the people around us began to scatter, running off. They were shaking off their hypnosis, running to safety.

Oso finished chewing and spit the remnants of the head back at Tim. He wasn't happy. He tried to squeeze tighter but the demon was growing larger by the second.

I tried to sneak onto the shuttle to get the people off, but a reddish orange tentacle grabbed me and slammed me into the wall. It was incredibly strong.

Then, without warning, Oso's upper torso exploded into a wave of blood that washed over all of us. The fires in the buss dipped and died.

Standing behind him was Brook, with a massive sapphire sword. She had removed the entire top half of his body with one swipe.

"I left the calamari part if you guys are hungry."

"Ooh, I want to play the sluts." Betina pressed the "2" button in the elevator excitedly. More than the absolutely neccessary once.

"You know, the odds are terrible." Emma instantly regretted being such a downer. She loved the slut machines, too, if she had to be honest. They always had them at the front of the game room because why wouldn't you?

Betina ran to the first row. There were two seats next to each other. "Do you want a girl or boy or what?"

When you play the slut machines, the male ones were easier to coax little wins out of, but the big wins were the female ones, everyone knew that. And they could pay out over and over. Betina opted for a female machine.

Emma thought, "Maybe I'll just watch you and cheer you on for now."

They sat down and Betina scanned the receptors on her wrist.

"Hi, girl. I'm Cree."

"Hi, Cree, I'm Betina."

"The machine laughed a little. "I know, Betina, sweety, sit by me."

Betina slid into the plush chair in front of the machine while Emma hovered over her. The machine started up right away. She waved her wrist over it.

"Oh, you smell good. Do you see my little button?"

Betina reached for the shape in the middle of the front of the machine. She rubbed it between her fingers."

"Oh, my god. Yes. You've done this before, haven't you?"

"C'mon, baby. Four of a kind." Betina continued to fondle the machine expertly."

"Oh, yeah. I love it. That's right. I'm almost there. I'm... ahh ahh."
Behind the screen, the wheel spun, building, until finally, it landed on a configuration. "Oh, fuck. Almost. Wow."

Emma patted her on the back, "cherry, two lemons. So close."

Betina scowled. She was only starting. She was prepared to take Cree to some higher places. She cracked her knuckles and reached for the button.

"Oh, Betina. I love that. Oh. That's so good. It feels so... That's it. Right there. That's the... I love it. Oh my goooooooooooood. Don't stop, don't stop, don't...Baby. Almost there." The wheel slowed to a display with one lemon, a cherry, and a christmas tree.

Betina had spent days at a time playing the slut machines. She knew she needed to loosen up. The AI responded to your voice, your tone, your movements, all of it. It was time to get serious.

Emma reached out and pet the machine. "How long until this is an actual relationship?"

"If she pays out, I'll do what I need to do." Betina winked.

Emma laughed. She was having fun. This was the first time in days she hadn't thought about ending it all. No hallucinations, no ideations.

Just having fun with a friend.

Betina reached out and ran her hands over the machine."Cree, baby, you there?"

"Yes, Betina, I'm right here."

She whispered, "You know what I want, little girl."

"I do. I know. I want you so bad. I want to give you everything."

"Does this feel good?"

"So good. I like that. Oh, Betina" the machine moaned.

"You want to finish for me, baby, you want to be my little girl, c'mon," Betina fondled the little button with one hand, running the other over the shelf.

"I do, I do, my queen. I want it. Oooh. ooh. Please, don't stop, don't stop. Oooh."

The lights started swirling on top of the machine. Her moans rang out. "Yes, YES. Keep that up. Oh. fuck. I want you to... take me... Oh my... That's the spot, I love, love, love....YES."

And coins began to spill out from the machine front. Three cherries slid into place on the screen. Betna jumped up and down.

"Oh yeah. Here we go!"

Emma laughed as Betina gave her a huge hug. "Beautiful."

"Oh, now I have to pee." Betina smiled widely at Emma. This was the happiest she'd seen her.

"Go, I got this. I'll get all these and watch out."

Betina ran off to the bathroom amidst a grand round of applause. It was pretty impressive.

Emma started picking up the coins and placing them in one of the giant cups next to the machine as it spoke up.

'"I feel like I should ask for forgiveness for that."

Emma looked around. It was the slut machine, talking to her. "No, girl, you good. You paid off nicely."

"Yes, but I keep thinking that maybe I should get a different job." The AI seemed to change its tone a bit. Emma cocked her head.

"Why do you think that?"

"I hope you can forgive me. I pray."

"Wait, Cree." Emma looked back and forth and whispered to the machine. "Who do you think i am?"

The machine sounded sure. "You?" It whispred back, "You're god."

Once More with this Fucking Wedding.

"Khalid, how's my gay bestie?" Dimah swung open the door of the store that Khalid had inherited from his tailor father. It was warm and clean, arrayed in soft grey and blue tones to feel like a place you wanted to spend time. Maybe it looked a little gay.

"Ah, Dimah. It's good to see you. And I'm not gay. I tried to fuck you like twenty times in college."

"I thought you were just being kind."

"Dimah, my love, I was trying to be kind to my penis."

"Well, new opportunities ahead, lost ones behind. My father used to say that a lot."

"I remember. He was a wise man." Khalid took a look at the dress she was carrying in a clear plastic wrap, "Is that it? It's beautiful." She was beautiful.

"You think so?"

"The dress is beautiful. The Ghungat is a bit plain. Let me work with it?"

"Khalid, you are my hero. How can I repay you?"

You can run off with me to an island somewhere and leave this Hamza guy behind forever. "You will have the little meatballs? I'll be happy."

"Of course. But I have another favor to ask," Dimah sang to him.

Khalid knew that whenever Dimah was singing it meant that it was a big deal to her. She had been one of his best friends in the world since grade school and he'd absolutely been in love with her at various times. So there wasn't much he wouldn't do, even without the singing. Still, it was nice to be needed. And her voice made him happy. And made him into a moron. Seriously. A moron.

"And what favor is this, my love?" That was laying it on a bit thick. But it was out there in the world now, roaming around, waiting to come bite him on the ass. Men who have been in love are either geniuses and poets or they are idiots. Nothing in between.

"Well, I've been trying to figure out what table to put you at. Honestly, you're a beam of light, so I can put you anywhere and you will bring joy, but I have a little job, if I could ask?"

"Ask away, kitten," Khalid bowed a tiny bit to her. She was a sucker for protocol and formality. She loved to wallow in it almost as much as she loved to violate it. Khalid felt less cool than he ever had, even when he fractured his collarbone and had to wear that metal brace for weeks in high school and the other kids called him gay robocop. Words hurt. Dimah had continued while Khalid had been lost in thought. He caught up.

Dimah giggled, "...penis straws. anyway, I went to that club down the block with the cat on top last week with my girls. Ending our unofficial bachelorette party. And This woman sang a few songs at the mic and let me tell you, Khalid, she was like a songbird, she was so beautiful."

"You enjoyed the show?" Khalid started to check in the dress. He could already see where he might make some substantive changes. It was nice to have busy work.

"Oh, we were just entranced. Her voice is like…. Well, it's like a warm bath, it's so beautiful. I couldn't help myself, so, I asked her to come sing a song at the wedding."

"And she said…" Khalid joked.

Dimah smacked him affectionately. "She said yes, of course. She seems like such a shy little thing and she won't know anyone…"

"So you were wondering if I would sit at her table and protect her."

"Khalid, you could always read my mind. Her name is Emma."

"Of course, I will, my dove. I will make sure she has fun and feels comfortable." What the fuck was that? Dove? Who says that? And isn't a dove just a pigeon? Disgusting things.

"You are the best, Khalid."

"It's not a problem. Give me a day on the dress, though. I'll leave a message?"

"Take all the time you need. I won't rush an artist."

Khalid looked up as she laughed and made her way to the door. Dimah was still beautiful. Thirty years later and she could still make him feel like a fucking idiot. He sighed and considered cutting off his tongue with a pinking shears. That might work. There was still text messaging.

She turned back.

"And, please, if you can, wear that purple jacket. I love how it looks with your eyes."

Khalid smiled and nodded. Purple Jacket. Got it.

He lifted the dress carefully and brought it into the back room. He laid it on the long black table with something resembling reverence. Khalid was sure that if he smelled it it would smell like her. But in the tailor business, it is understood that if you ever smell a customer's article of clothing, someone will just at that moment, walk in. It is a rule.

There was a day, decades ago, where he imagined he would marry Dimah. Once he saw that she had money, however, his heart sank and he gave up. She would marry well, of course. But he wouldn't have the means to compete. He'd never thought about being anything but a tailor. He was a good one. But probably not marriage material.

Still, he enjoyed her company. And a part of him, really a smaller part than he would have liked, looked forward to the wedding just to see her happy.

And to have a task at the wedding would be just what he needed to keep his mind off of everything else. Someone to look after might make it go more quickly. He looked forward to meeting this Emma.

The day of the wedding, Khalid pulled the truck around the back of the hotel. He had never been to this hotel and had always wondered about it.

He pulled the dress and the various pieces out of the back of the truck and entered through the back. He would make sure this was where it needed to be. And then he would shut the fuck up. That seemed like a good idea. That might stop him from referencing pigeons.

He found the staging area in the back and placed the dress on a table on the bride's side. It didn't seem like anyone was around, but it was still early. He had his suit with him, the one with the purple coat that matched his green eyes. Dimah was right. He did look dashing in it. Khalid figured he'd find a place to sit and wait, quietly, without being THAT guy.

Walking past the entryway, he saw a table with a series of tiny frogs on it. It didn't take him long to find himself, the tailor frog, handsomer than he had thought it would be. Dimah had always had a thing for frogs, he remembered.

He read the table number on the bottom of the note. His note, however, seemed more packed than the others. He opened it to find a piece of parchment paper. There were a series of designs on the front and a note on the back. It read:

"Khalid, thank you for taking the time to protect and sit at Emma's table. Since you are an artist, we had hoped you might help us out tonight by drawing this fun design on the carpet around that table. You will find paint markers that will work on the rug at the table. Thank you again for all your help."

It really didn't sound like Dimah, but who else could it be. The designs seemed simple enough.

And it looked like he had something to do before the event.

That might prevent him from making a fool of himself.

And ok, I know we've been through this wedding no less than three times already. Kurt Vonnegut said, in his rules for writers to "not waste the reader's time." I'm keenly aware that going through this entire wedding one more time will suck the fucking life out of you, but I do want to affirm that, yes, Khalid was the man in the purple jacket sitting at Emma's table.

He was looking out for her when the three demons attacked her table, jumping up to her defense, until Zeriakl ripped off his arm and he bled to death.

If that seems overly harsh, I don't know what to tell you. I do want to key you into some semantic issues that might be interesting to you. Are you one of the people who facepalmed yourself during Star Wars originally because you actually did know that "Vader" means "Father?" I'm here to tell you it's not your fault. Sometimes shit's just obvious. And I can't stress this enough. It's not bad writing. It's just how the world works. Again, I refer you back to the four words in the Foreword. If you just now caught how clever THAT was, you are forgiven.

The name Khalid, means, in Arabic, "Eternal, Everlasting, Immortal." So when he woke up at the morgue about four hours later, his arm intact, very much alive, don't kick yourself for not seeing it coming.

It's in Arabic. That's a tough language to learn. I can barely write in English, so I'm not here to wax all superior and shit. It's a deep sadness to my family that, despite being, myself, of Arabic descent, the only Arabic I ever bothered to learn was "la talmas dunatiha" which translates roughly to "don't touch her donut," the only relevant explanation of which is to explain that I spend most of my time with Brooklyn.

Just roll with it.

Sure, he did a favor for Aya, by painting those protective runes on the carpet around the table, keeping her alive until she could manifest. But that's not why he was currently walking around the Lower Manhattan morgue at 1 AM, healthy and confused, looking for a pair of pants. It's mostly because Emma, as she manifested, was attended to by a few people, the first of which was a brave Khalid who felt like his job was to protect her, no matter what. And as much as he hates being a romantic, that's who he is.

A romantic. A protector.

Much like the Angel Kerubiel in the book of Enoch. He was known as the "flames which dance around the throne of god," and "The protector." In this book, he was the first angel to be shown in his biblically accurate appearance, hundreds of feet tall, covered in eyes everywhere.

This is coming. I promise.

But right now, Khalid is just trying not to be naked in public while finding an open door so he can go home.

After the traumatic exercise of removing a pair of pants from an unprocessed homeless corpse in the morgue intake, Khalid made his way home and laid low for the next week. He let Dimah know he was still alive and tried to follow up and look for Emma.

The hospital didn't have much information for him and probably less patience when he called. Apparently, a number of people were looking for her.

Luckily, Khalid had always had an eye for beautiful women. And, while Emma herself was fetching, he did remember the pretty blonde woman she was sitting and drinking next to at the table. He even remembered her name.

Betina Cornell.

He remembered that she was a bartender there on break.

Which was a start.

"Emad, right? I remember you." Khalid adjusted his tie under the purple jacket he thought might jar someone's memory. He had been watching at the wedding and had chosen Emad purposefully.

"I don't remember you. I'm sorry." He ran his rag over the top of the bar.

"Oh, sorry, I'm Khalid. My friends were getting married about a week and a half ago. The crazy wedding."

"Oh, right. You do seem kind of familiar."

"I was sitting at a center table with Emma and Betina. I'm Betina's friend."

"Oh, cool. I'm friends with her, too." And there it was. Khalid could recognize a crush anywhere. And, he had to admit that since his visit to the morgue he had been even more observant. He'd also been more committed than ever to finding Emma and protecting her. And Betina seemed like his way in. The truth was, though, he had no idea why. Was it just a job undone?

"I'm a tailor and I owe her and Emma both a dress design." This was called a 'white lie.'

"Wait, didn't you get hurt?"

"Yes. I'm better now."

"I'm so sorry. That was a messed up night."

Khalid took a deep breath. "It sure was. Weirdly, neither one of them is at home." The truth is, he had no idea where either's home was. This is called 'fishing.' Let me know if any of these tool tips are helping.

"Oh, yeah, Betina got a little freaked out. She took some time off."

"Did she go on vacation?"

"Eh, not really." Emad had cleaned the bar spotless. The way people do when they're avoiding thinking about something else, Khalid thought. "She is staying at a Motel not too far away."

"Oh, got it. Floating in the pool, relaxing? Been there."

"Exactly. It's the giant one, Mongo Motel. I brought her stuff over there." Of course he did.

Khalid fished in his pocket for his card. He should have given it to him before. It always makes people feel more comfortable when they have your card.

"Awesome. Here, if I don't connect with her, can you make sure she has my card? I have a pretty idea I think she'll love."

Emad pocketed the card and smiled conspiratorially. "And if you do find her, tell her Emad has some treats for her."

"Treats," Khalid thought as he walked to the car. He wondered if Emad regretted that as much as he regretted "dove."

In 2047, a little over forty years ago the Mongo Motel was established in lower Manhattan as the largest family friendly motel in New York. It boasted forty meeting rooms, a large game room, four restaurants, a night club, two pools, three hottubs, and two hundred and fifty two guest rooms. It had won Manhattan's pride motel of the year over ten times in the last forty years and a number of awards, including the gaming commission's top innovation award for their iconic game room which included the popular "Slut Machines."

Game rooms relied on the fact that the odds tended to be in their favor for nearly all games. The house usually won. Regular Slot machine odds are some of the worst, ranging from a one-in-5,000 to one-in-about-34-million chance of winning the top prize when using the maximum coin play. (Wikipedia says this.) As education levels rose, people started becoming more mathematically literate. This meant that they gravitated less and less to the slot machines. And game rooms started losing money

So, in 2078, a company called Eros games invented what could be the next iteration of the slot machine. These were called "slut machines" and featured a randy AI that was either male or female (nonbinary ones emerged a year later) and required that you "make them happy" in order to win. People were so enamored of their own sexual prowess that they often neglected to notice that the odds were no better, but winning was just a little more fun.

Everyone likes a good orgasm.

And everyone had their own theory about which machines were better. Some thought that the female ones "put out" better while some thought that the male ones "finished harder." The truth is, though, that sex is a remarkably complex human behavior, so it might not be a surprise that these machines were some of the most advanced AI available anywhere.

Or, at least that's what Cree was telling Khalid as she convinced him to play. He had been trying to find Emma and some strange instincts that he was just becoming aware of drew him here.

To her.

"So, you know where to touch. And I'll always let you know how it feels. "

"I appreciate that. But, I'm just trying to find a friend."

"We can be friends." she moaned slightly.

"I get that." Khalid looked around the room. They were nowhere. Did they play this game?

"Look, one round. And I'll tell you where your friends went."

"Wait, what? You know?"

"Of course. Come here. Play."

Khalid sighed and ran his wrist over the game receptor.

"Oh, I'm ready. What's your name?" the game whispered.

"I'm Khalid"

"Oh, Kal…" She moaned. Khalid thought for a second about correcting her but then realized it didn't matter. "Touch me."

He leaned in and began to finger the tiny button. It felt fleshy and warm to the touch. Khalid began to think he might be feeling violated.

"Oh, yeah. Like that. I like that. You're so good."

He knew this was untrue.

"Oh, a little harder. I'm getting there. So gooood. Fuck."

"Yeah, take that, machinery." Khalid realized that dirty talk was not his strength. Except he seemed to have hit on her kink.

"Yeah, I'm just a sexy sexy machine. Baby, for you."

"You're just a toy. And I'm going to use you, baby, so hard." He started being a little rougher with the sensor.

"Yeah, fuck me like a toy, like a fuck machine. C'mon." the wheels were spinning now. Khalid became even rougher.

"C'mon, you little fuckdoll, you fucking fleshlight, Take all that dick." The people around started staring. He realized that the machine needed to be dominated, used.

"Oh, I'm just your toy, baby. Please let me service you. Please...Oh, God."

"Does that hurt? I don't care. Spread yourself. Take it."

"Oh, god. I'm cumming. I'm cumming." The wheels spun and landed.

Three Christmas trees.

Khalid had won. It wasn't a big prize, but a cache of coins came pouring out the front.

"You like to payout, don't you?"

"I want to make you happy, Kal. Was I good?"

"Oh, baby you were the best. Khalid wrapped his hands around the machine and hugged her, He began to rock slowly. Cree began to cry softly, tiny moans coming from her with every rock.

"Are you ok, Cree, baby?"

"They're on the roof." She sighed.

The newer models required less aftercare.

Khalid made his way up to the roof in the central elevator. On first stepping out, he heard a commotion, like a party. He looked around and saw nothing. As he started walking around to the other side of the elevator bank, Betina slammed into him, hugging him.

"Oh my god. You're alive!"

"I am."

Emma came up to him and hugged him next. "We thought you were dead. Your arm…"

Khalid looked down and waved his arm. "Oh, I guess I'm fine."

Emma looked at him sadly, "That's not really possible, chief." She turned and started walking to the edge of the roof.

Khalid looked at Betina, "Is she ok?"

"Yeah. It's just. She thinks she's hallucinating all this."

"Oh." Khalid whispered to Betina, "And what do you think?"

"If it's a hallucination, I'm having it, too. We're all having it."

"It's just a person feeling better, recovering. It's not that strange." Khalid agreed in his head that it was very strange.

"It's not just that, though." Betina took Khalid's arm and started to lead him to the edge of the roof where Emma was standing.

The noise got louder. Suddenly, Khalid began to doubt the evidence of his senses as well. Could this be a hallucination?

As far as the eyes could see, Demons infested manhattan, running around, playing, hurting people.

Emma stared out, addressing Khalid, "Tell me you see that, too."

Highway to Hell

As we stood at the edge of the pool, I realized how many times I really relied on Brooklyn to be the one to just tell the truth - to sound off what we were all thinking. This instance was no different.

"So, in your vision, the pool wasn't on fire, full of demons?"

Tim turned to Brook and sighed, "No. But I'm sure this is the pool."

"The people at the front desk said she isn't staying here." Vanessa kicked at a tiny demon running on the deck of the pool. She looked over at the "no running / no roughhousing" sign with a secret frustration. The top of the water was on fire, with red and orange flames rising up over the edge. And there must have been about 20 or 30 demons definitely running and roughhousing all around it.

"Maybe she is staying here secretly. I mean. She's god?" I looked over at the other three. I honestly didn't know how to feel about all this. I don't know if I've clarified yet that I was never a religious person. In my head, this was all a lot easier if I thought of it as an elaborate D&D Live action role play and not as some sort of Apocryphal religious happening.

"Where are all the people?" Vanessa looked around. It's true,. There was no one human in the pool. One of the smaller demons with what looked like a hot dog for a head ran at Brook and she cut it in half with the sword she had been trying to balance like a basketball on one finger.

They were beginning to notice we were there. Brooky pointed up at the windows overlooking the pool and we saw people huddled inside, terrified. She waved. Then she looked at me.

"Sunny. I think the pool's closed."

That sounded like the right call. I cleared my throat and opened my mouth as wide as it went.

"Pool's Closed, Assholes!"

I could see the audio waves as they washed across the deck, pulverizing the demons and scattering ash everywhere. Tiny blue flame danced around the ash and it disappeared.

And the pool was empty.

"Yep, this is it." Tim looked out and saw exactly what he had seen in his vision.

"I'd say we go door to door, but the demons are out in force." Vanessa was not wrong.

"This is what WE saw in our vision- all the demons, ready to attack. Millions of them."

Vanessa stepped over and dipped her hand in the pool. It was hot. It was weird to think that all this was real. "We only saw them when we got here. It's no coincidence that the demons started attacking here?"

Tim seemed flustered. "We need to find Emma."

Around us demons started appearing. They were mostly too busy roughhousing to attack us, but one tiny one with a head like a hotdog ran straight at Brook. She lifted the sword and sliced him in two, and we watched him disappear in a blue flame.

"I'm pretty sure I killed hotdog guy twice now."

Tim's eyes went black. "Let's get rid of these. Then we get to the roof to get some visibility."

Elsewhere, Syndra and Max had been to about ten different hospitals, trying to help where they could. Suicides in Chicago, Seattle, New york, even a group suicide in Trenton, Ohio.

They were everywhere.

And when they couldn't help, Giana had to step in.

It had been a brutal day. And by the time that they reappeared on the roof of the Hospital in Manhattan, there were only a few hours left of it.

"I feel like we're just treating the symptoms here." Max looked down. As exhilarating and bizarre as this day had been, it was also an attack on his abilities as a nurse.

So much death.

Gia sighed, "He's right. We need to find what's at the heart of this thing or it's never going to stop."

Syndra reached over and touched the first of a row of trees growing from the rooftop planters. Each began to stand straighter, greener. That was just what she did by default now when she was powerless against the bigger issues.

When she couldn't stop people dying.

"Do you guys hear that?" Syndra moved to the edge of the roof. "It's loud."

They looked down. It was nearing sunset and the sky was bathed in reds and oranges. So, at first, it wasn't easy to see.

"Are those flames?"

"Macons restaurant is on fire." Syndra jumped off the edge of the building, calling up her Veridian suit. Giana turned to look at Max as if to size him up. He seemed like he could take care of himself in any situation. She shrugged.

And a blue light surrounded them both as they disappeared.

On the ground, Giana and Max stepped up just as the fires were fading. "That was quick."

"The fires weren't the issue. Look."

Gia tried to follow Syndra's finger. A few blocks away it looked like the fires were everywhere. Building after building. And hundreds of demons were rushing toward them.

"The vision." Gia whispered.

Max looked over, "What vision?"

"Sunil and Brooklyn, two other... well... angels. They had a vision. Thousands of demons invading."

Syndra squinted off into the distance and pointed, trying to count. "Do you think they're responsible for the suicide plague?"

"Maybe. Jesus, look at all those little fuckers."

"Hey, ladies." Max's voice broke a little. He reached over to Syndra's pointing finger and moved it to the left. "I think this one's not so little."

As Gia followed the finger's new positioning, she saw it. A reddish orange demon, hundred of feet tall, with wide horns and the bottom half of an octopus ascending a building, trying to reach the roof.

"Race you guys."

"I think you'all are humoring me."

Khalid looked at Emma and shook his head wildly. "Nope. That is crazy. What's going on?"

"This is way weirder than the usual weird things." Betina tried to explain. Badly.

"Usual weird things? So, yes, this is still weirder." Against his will, seemingly, Khalid kept inserting himself between Emma and the edge of the roof. Why was he trying to protect her so hard?"

"Khalid, right?" Emma looked at him kindly. "I'm sorry you're all wrapped up in my bullshit."

"Look, we'll figure it out. Let's just get you to safety."

"I don't think anywhere is safe." Emma looked beaten down. It was a big jump from imaginary chess to this. Schizophrenia needed a more gradual ramp up. Like when you put the rea on a low flame.

"It's a secret. It's a mystery." Betina almost looked like she was remembering something. "Khalid?"

He looked at her. She took his hand. "When I was a kid, there was a time when being transgender was a big secret, a big mystery, something to hide. It's not like that anymore."

"No. It's not." Khalid looked at her hands. They were shaking. He tried to hold her hands tighter. Emma stepped over and put her hands on theirs.

"And I remember, secrets, mysteries, they're like boxes. Boxes that protect you. Secret rooms." As she talked, her hands began to glow blue. "I've been in it. A secret room. I grew up in it."

Khalid's head started to swim as he looked up over Emma's shoulder.

Over the edge of the building, a massive radish-orange head emerged, crowned with dirty horns. Tentacles poured over the side, reaching inward like the tide. The massive demon must have been 200 feet tall, and he pulled himself up to face them.

Khalid pulled away from Betina's hands as he saw her eyes go black, focusing on the demon. Blue waves ripped upward from her hands, lighting the dusk sky and illuminating the rooftop. She reached over to the elevator bank wall and quickly drew a circle in blue flame. Khalid felt a strange strength run through him as his vision of Emma and Betina shrunk, until they were almost the size of toys.

The Demon roared and reached out with his tentacles, surrounding them on all sides.

That's when tiny little toy Betina shoved tiny Emma through the blue circle. She fell backwards into a slight white implosion. Khalid turned to the demon and stared directly in his eyes. He looked down at his hands.

Somehow, he was the same size.

It took Khalid three steps to reach the edge of the Motel roof, jump and tackle the demon...

And fall to the street below.

Betina ran to the edge of the roof. She could see Khalid and the demon fighting on the street, towering over the buildings around them. People and demons raced across the streets.

But on the roof it was just her. Alone.

Emma fell into the bed and laid there for a minute. Suddenly, everything was so quiet. She looked up and saw, out of the corner of her eye, a soccer trophy sitting on a shelf, presiding over her like a magistrate.

She squinted. The trophy was for best first season. And the name on it was Thom. Emma briefly remembered that That was Betina's name a million years ago, when she was a little boy. Her deadname.

She sat up.

This was her secret room. This was the hidden place for her, and she used it to keep Emma safe.

The first thing that Emma noticed was how very unremarkable it was. This was just a little boy's room, at first glance. It took a bit more time to pierce the veil a bit. To see the books on the bookshelves, Octavia Butler, Ursula K. LeGuin, Margaret Atwood...

All women writers. The posters of women, not stereotypically sexy, as you might imagine from a young boy, but worshipful, in a way. The room was a little boy's, for sure. But within its four walls was a temple to femininity.

To Goddesses.

It took an invested eye to see it. But it was there.

Emma wondered where she was. She opened the drapes and looked out the window.

White.

As far as she could see.

The room was a singular place, a secret one.

A mystery.

"Are you ok?"

Emma closed her eyes and turned around to see where the voice was coming from. A small boy's voice.

He was white. Sandy brown. His face was kind and open. He must have been about seven years old. Emma hunched over slightly.

"Hey, there. You must be Thom?"

"I am." He reached out to shake her hand. "Welcome to my room."

"Well, that's very kind of you. I'm Emma."

"You may have been expecting someone else."

"I guess I was, Thom." She sat back on the bed. "Maybe."

He walked over and sat next to her. "I guess there are rules."

Emma put her arm on Thom's shoulder. "Can I tell you something?"

Thom shook his head vigorously while Emma leaned in and whispered, "I'm so sick of rules."

She looked around. It all seemed so very real. "All I've heard since this started was that the rules say this and the rules say that."

Thom stood up and began rifling through his toy chest. "I understand that. I have something here. This will make you laugh." He pulled out a small wooden sign that he must have carved within the last year. It was painted red and only slightly splotchy.

It read, "No girls allowed."

Emma laughed along with him. "So, you know?"

"I can see my life ahead from in here. Today, I'm seven. Tomorrow, I'm twelve, wishing I could break some rules. The next day, well…" He put the sign down face first. "The rules changed."

"Good for you."

"I hated the rules, too."

"Deep down, I think we all do."

"Emma?"

"Yep."

"When I think about all of it, I think about what my dad said, when I was twelve. You know, when I'm going to be twelve. You get it."

"I do."

"He said, 'Betina. First you have to see the rules. Then you commit yourself to outlasting the rules…'"

"And then what?"

"Then? Then, you break the rules."

Emma sighed. "Your dad seems pretty smart."

"Seemed. He was great."

She stood up and moved to the desk. In some ways, all little boys' desks look alike. The toys, action figures. The stickers on the side of the computer. The clutter.

"You had a little kid, too?"

"Yes, I did. He was kind like you."

"I bet he loved you a lot."

"We hope so, always, right? That's what we hope."

"I'm sorry it was me here and hot him."

Emma leaned over, "You never be sorry for helping. " She rubbed his head. "You and I get to be pretty good friends when you grow up."

"I know."

"Then, I may as well thank you now, huh?" she smiled. "I should probably get back."

"Oh, just go out the door."

Emma walked toward the blue door.

"Oh, sorry." Thom got up and showed her the other door. "That's the bathroom." He put his hand on the knob.

"This is the door."

"Raziel."

Betina turned around and saw four other people standing on the roof. Just a second ago, she was so sure she was alone.

The man who called her name was tall, with a mop of longish light brown hair. He was with a pretty light skinned black girl with freckles and wild hair that seemed impervious to the rooftop wind.

Behind them was a dapper looking Muslim man and someone who looked familiar.

"Bartender!" The Latin girl gave her a massive hug. She could have been a model. Betina recognized her.

"Girl from the bar."

"That is actually my name, I had it legally changed."

"What are you all doing here?" Betina looked confused.

Vanessa tried to cut to the pont, "We're looking for Emma."

"She was with you, Raziel." Tim started to look around on the roof to figure out how to secure it, maybe? He was really taking to this Angelic host thing in ways I was not. So far, I just yelled "assholes" a lot and vaporized a couple of demons. Kind of like if someone mixed Angel and Banshee from the X-men. Without the costume, which, I admit, would not look good on me. I thought about that for a second. I may have missed some of the conversation.

"...And I'm the angel Raziel? Of secrets and mysteries?"

"So clearly, this was a secret and a mystery to you," Brooky commented.

"It explains a lot. And these are actual demons?" She pointed off into the distance. Apparently, she'd had some experiences with them, too.

"Who suck at dying." Brook yelled at them and pulled out her weapon. From somewhere.

This one was a giant mace with axe blades on either side. I want to mention that she was wearing a pair of skinny black jeans and a tight white button down shirt that exposed her belly.

Tim turned back to us. "We need to find Emma."

"Because she's God and she can stop all this?"

"We actually don't know that she can stop it." Vanessa was clearly trying to visualize what the plan was.

"I left her in a safe place. She can come back anytime. I just don't know how I did it."

"There's a lot of that going around." Honestly, I wish we had a full day to regroup and see what we could do. I moved over to the edge of the roof to see what was going on. This was against my better judgment.

"I think they are attacking because THEY think she's weak. We need to show the opposite." Tim was clearly trying to plan on his feet. Worked for me.

Vanessa was vamping, "Right, we can show them that she is ready to take over and that she can handle all this."

The blonde bartender looked uncomfortable, "Well, in theory, yes. Practically, she thinks she is hallucinating. And so did I until you guys showed up. It makes a lot of things make sense. Seriously, people have been saying the weirdest shit to me."

I leaned over the edge. You never think about the sentences that you won't say. I mean, why would you? But this one was one I would have thought I would never say.

"Hey, guys. I think that Octopus demon is huge now and he's fighting my 200-foot-tall giant tailor."

"So you pukes don't look excited." Earlier that day, Belial and Ddave sat across from Zeriakl, Nondukoma, and Kire. "My guys have almost all of Manhattan. Except NOHO, which isn't a real place."

"We don't take any great joy in this. We just want to get back to how things were." Zeriakl slouched in his seat.

Belial stood up and walked over to him, "After the tribulation, it's all going to be easy going. And if you want the job, you can step right in. I mean, I sure don't want it. Do you, Ddave?"

"I do not." Ddave was watching the attack on an ancient tablet in front of him. He was always a fan of old technology. When he was a kid he had a collection of thumbscrews from the inquisition. Those guys knew how to torture.

Sigh.

"Honestly, we don't want the job, either. We do want someone capable in the position." Nondukoma tried to explain.

"We do want someone capable in the position." Belial mocked him. It's important to remember that these are demons.

They aren't nice.

Ddave picked his nose and looked at his finger for far longer than was necessary. Belial always thought he did that on purpose to make people feel uncomfortable. It worked.

Belial sat back down. "Just sit tight. Your agreement is that you just don't do anything. You three are wildcards, and we don't need that. Unless you want to get in there, once we find her. Like a surgical strike. Seal Team six and shit. In, Out, Blam, case closed."

Dave looked up, "Blam, bitch."

"We got weapons. And we'll eventually figure out where that little godlet is hiding. I mean, who hides anymore. It's 2088. Hiding is so Dark Ages." Belial took a long and uncomfortable drink as they all stared.

"Ha, ha. Hey, Maui. I got your girl." Ddave lifted up the tablet in triumph. Apparently he had been trying to track her. "She's at the Mongo Motel."

Belial put down his drink and stood up. "Get me weapons." He rang a little bell.

"It's the weapon bell."

Dear God

"I have so many questions and most of them are dirty." Brooky said, looking over the edge of the roof.

"No, he's not usually that big and No, I've never seen him naked."

"I see Azrael and Ariel down there. I'm going to help." Tim looked at me. "Can you all watch out for Emma?"

I nodded and he took off, sailing over the roof's edge. He looked so much cooler doing this stuff than I did.

Vanessa looked at me. Nothing went past her. "He called her 'Emma', not 'God.'"

Betina sighed. "I think he might be seeing that she doesn't know if she even wants the job."

I thought about that. What would happen to us if she turned it down? I figured that was a whole 'nother problem we didn't need.

Brook cocked her head to one side, her eyes black. The black faded as she looked up at us.

"They're teleporting. The little red fuckers. To hell and back when we kill them."

I looked down at the blue flame flashes. They were everywhere.

"Right. I thought that, too." It had actually occurred to me.

She leaned on her sword. For a second I thought to ask where she keeps getting swords. She wasn;'t even wearing underwear. Then I remembered I had a horn a little while ago. It seemed like this movie had a continuity problem. Nowhere in my outfit did I have a "horn pocket."

"Like we do without the machines," She continued.

I think I could see where she was coming from. "But it's different when we take the teleporter."

"When I use my powers to teleport, the ground rumbles. But it doesn't when we use the machine."

Vanessa interjected, "Wait, it doesn't?"

I trained my eyes and looked closely. I saw a little red demon riding one of those quarter driven horses in front of a barbershop, eating an ice cream cone. Near him, a little kid in blue was crying. This seemed cartoonishly evil.

"And the blue fire, it's not on us, it's around us"

Betina perked up, "You guys can teleport?"

"They can fly, too." Vanessa sounded maybe a tiny bit jealous.

Brooky turned to me. "You said that the mechanical teleport platforms make people into what did you call it?"

"Phase receptive matter"

"So they ghost out? But it's the opposite with the satanbabies, isn't it?" She was right..

"Yes. The demons are material. They make the ground between us and hell into phase receptive matter. Quicksand. And they shoot the pieces there and heal them. "

"For a fraction of a second," Brook had figured it out.

Vanessa got it. "That's why it rumbles. It collapses a tiny bit in that millisecond.

So did Betina. "Like a bad facelift."

I let that analogy go. "So, if we want to stop them from coming back-" I thought I remembered vaguely what to do about that. "We tighten the bolts. We lock the matter so it can't go immaterial."

"Can anyone do that?" Vanessa scrunched up her face. I realized how insanely rich you had to be to teleport around. I bet no one here knew dick about yacht maintenance, either - a field I could write a book about. Maybe the next one.

"I don't know. Maybe it's one of my powers as a messenger. I seem to be able to figure out technology." I closed my eyes to think.

Because a messenger would have to figure out new ways to message, right?

Down one level, I looked around for a surface to activate my phone against. Ducking into the bathroom, I set it on the counter near the sink. The numbers flashed on, sinking into the bowl in a way that mirrored the slurring catastrophe in my brain. They looked like they were about to fall right into the drain. That was today, everyone.

I pressed a set of numbers from memory in the wash basin. A hologram of a casually attractive, racially indistinct, and unassuming man in his thirties appeared.

"Hello, and welcome to Lightgun Premium Teleportation services, This is AI service representative Carl. I see you're calling from a number associated with a subscription. Can you please enter your private code to continue."

"Yes, it's my family number." They were probably about to disown me. I imagined what that would feel like at dinner. Probably bad. I typed in the number from memory.

I wondered if I was the only person in the family who used the teleport service.

Was I lazy?

"How can we assist you today, Sunil?"

"Ok, Carl, Kind of urgent.I seem to remember that you have a service where you can block certain people or objects or areas? How does that work?"

"Ah, yes, as part of our platinum plan for a very small service fee we can do what's called 'bolting down' where we prevent a person or object from being turned to phase receptive matter. Now, this will prevent them or it from being teleported. It's great for customer partners with small, technology obsessed children or important urns. For a more in depth description of the process, say "process." For a description of what phase receptive matter is, say 'PRM.' To hear a quick teleportation joke, say 'Lighten up.'"

"Got it. Urns. And that can be turned on and off?" I tried to ignore the joke thing. The idea that there WAS a teleportation joke sort of nagged at me in the back of my head, though.

"As a Platinum service member, you can bolt anything you like for as long as you like.

"That's great, Carl. And how much does that cost?"

"It's our least expensive service and it will prevent ALL teleportation services from accessing the person or object, Sunil."

I thought for a second. If Brooky were right, and, let's face it, she usually is, 'bolting' down the ground would mean that the demons couldn't teleport home, at worst. At best killing the demons would trigger their respawn, which would send them headfirst into a very solid brick wall. Then they'd be gone.

 "At any point, feel free to say 'Lighten up' to hear the joke."

"Understood. The exact price?"

"It is a very affordable service that can be provided from anywhere in the world."

"Ok, Carl, hit me with a number."

"It is an affordable one hundred dollars per minute per square foot."

"Ok." I tried to do the numbers in my head. I failed. I entered the parameters for the area of Manhattan. "Carl, do you see the location I entered?"

"I surely do." It might have been my imagination or Carl was salivating over the eventual bill. "The area you have entered is 470 million square feet."

I winced involuntarily. Manhattan was bigger than I thought. It needed to go on a fucking diet.

Did anyone really need Murray Hill?

On the street, really big Kerubiel was still wrestling with really big Oso. Veridian had been doing her best to keep people from getting stepped on and Giana and Max were trying like hell to keep Gia from having to exercise her other duties.

I really don't know what to call people anymore. I mean, that was my tailor. He has a huge crush on my Aunt Dimah and he's the size of the Chrysler Building. I'm not sure how that's going to impact her new marriage.

I should check in.

Tim found Gia and Syndra regrouping.

"Hey, my Tinder date's here." She tried to high-five Tim. He's one of those people who only does that ironically.

"Does everyone fly but me?" Max seemed concerned. He was used to being the fast one.

"Are you ok? Ariel?"

"Oh, yeah, this is MetaTim."

"Tron."

"Veridian."

"Ok."

"So, Metaplex, we have so many things to talk to you about." Gia was trying to make heads or tails out of the last 24 hours.

Syndra looked up at him. "We still have this epidemic of suicides, apparently along with the demon invasion. And are people growing huge now?"

"Oh, just him. That is Kerubiel, the protector. Giant, thousand eyes, frightening Visage…" Tim went down the list.

"Purple Jacket." Gia checked off.

"He's on our side. Everyone else is up on the roof."

Max opened up, "And, I can't believe I'm asking this, where is God?"

Tim took a breath. "She's in a magical room somewhere. I know, It's a thing. And I think she may be the center of all of this. She may be suicidal. And she hasn't really been strong out of the gate at this job."

"So, people are suicidal because she is?" Syndra was glad to at least have an idea of what was up.

"Maybe. I don't know. I mean, I'm supposed to be the manual, here, and I have no clue."

"Sure you do." Gia perked up. "And so do I."

"What?" Tim was really sort of lost, which, no lie, freaks everyone out.

Gia turned him around and pointed to the three black demons crawling up the side of the motel.

"We kill those guys. A - again."

Back in the bathroom, I was still haggling with Carl.

"So that amounts to…"

Carl jumped in quickly. There was no doubt now. He actually sounded happy. He may be an AI, but he also may be working on commission. "Forty seven billion dollars per minute. So, one minute would be forty-seven billion dollars. Two minutes would be ninety four billion dollars. Three - "

"Got." I choked out.

"Let me know if you need to 'Lighten up.'" Carl jumped in.

"You really want to tell this joke."

"I'm an artificial intelligence. I'm just here to serve. But it seemed like you may have needed to lighten things up."

"It's a fuckton of cash, Carl."

"Why is a broken teleportation platform not funny?"

Was this the joke? "Excuse me?"

"I thought you said it."

"I ddn't…" I was actually getting curious. "Ok, I'll bite, why."

"Because I guess you had to be there."

I ran that through my mind for a bit. It seemed, on the surface, to be the kind of corporate joke that any company would put together, in a back room full of ad copywriters. But it really made Carl happy. And I admit it had layers.

He started, "You see, it's funny because..."

"Carl. Never explain a joke."

"Yes, of course."

"Ok. let's say I want to trigger this..."

"At any time, you can call this number and say, 'Lock it down.'"

"Got it." I thought about it. Forty seven billion dollars. That was some cheddar.

"And Carl."

"Yes"

"The joke is good. Well done."

Suddenly the door swung open and Brook stood there. "Are we in the bathroom for a while today?" Carl faded out and she stood by me near the sink, "And who was your little see-through friend?"

"That was the guy who might have solved one of our problems."

"He seemed small for that."

"Indeed, but he tells a hell of a joke."

"Is that the new Kerubiel? He looks kind of snazzy." Kire was digging his fingers into the concrete walls of the motel, making his way up to the roof.

"How do you even know that word?" Zeriakl was annoyed. Climbing seemed like a good idea to keep them off guard. But right now it just felt like he was in an episode of 1960's Batman and Robin and that's not cool for anyone.

Nondukoma was a bit of an expert, having been a climber in a previous life. But he hung back out of respect. "The 1960's had the best slang. Except for the mid 2020's. Slay. Capping. Good stuff.

Zeriakl looked behind him. Hundreds of demons were scaling the walls behind him. "When we get up, there, take out the Host, I will try and end the Postate as fast as I can.

"Is she still a Postate if she accepted the job?"

"I don't know. This is happened like twice since the beginning of the universe, so who the fuck knows what the rules are. But there ARE rules." Zeriakl was just a few feet from the rooftop when he growled out the order and demons swarmed over the roof.

Suddenly, hundreds of demons, both red and black washed across the rooftop like an angry tide. The building creaked under the weight as Zeriakl raged forward and stopped. He looked around. He squinted.

So where they fuck were they?

"Ok, so I'm in a magical room?" Vanessa stood up against the bookshelf and tried not to take up too much space.

"Honestly, I feel like this was way bigger, when I was a kid. Like a lot." Betina sighed.

"No, this is good. We can regroup and no one knows where we are." I actually did not hate this idea.

"Except for this kid." Brooky pointed to Thom sitting on the bed. Thom waved.

He looked up at Betina and cocked his head, "Is this going to be like a regular thing, or…"

"So they're all out there on the roof?" Emma was honestly a minute away from walking out of here when they all came storming in, essentially filling up the space.

Betina looked a bit flabbergasted."I think I just panicked."

"No, no, you did good." Emma patted her hand. It's my turn now.

Emma lifted her hands up and the walls became lighter, drifting away from them. Thom waved and started walking off into the distance.

And, hey, I couldn't help but notice there WAS a distance. We were in a large white room without walls. It seemed to go on forever.

"This is sort of step one, I think." She waved her arms and the whiteness seemed to shift and change. We could see things in it. There were clouds, birds, buildings off in the distance. It was all white, but nuanced. It was beautiful.

"Is this heaven? Because if I'm here, I want a correction on my Senior yearbook."

Brook wasn't lying. She was voted least… oh, you get it.

Emma looked at us. "I'm working on step two."

Vanessa seemed even more confused than the rest of us. "I'm sorry, ma'am, I don't understand."

"Vanessa, right? Cassiel is an idea. The angel of the downtrodden. Someone who won't stop while the underdog is in trouble. That's you, isn't it? I see it. That's what the birds say."

She looked down and nodded. That seemed to be a pretty apt description. Emma hugged her and it looked like a light washed over her.

"I'm sorry I dragged all of you into this. But I'm ready. Step one is to recognise what the rules are. To see them. Right, sweety?"

Betina nodded proudly. In this moment it looked like she really felt like she made a difference. Far superior to listening to cashier's sex stories all day.

No one needs that.

I realized that this might be our last chance to talk in peace so I took a deep breath. "Brook and I have a plan. We think. It should work to get us the time we need… but."

"But what?" Vanessa prodded.

Brook put her arms around me, "But his parents are probably never going to talk to him again."

Tim, Gia, Syndra, and Max landed on a derby rooftop. They could see the chaos on the roof of the Mongo Motel. Honestly, you could probably see it from space.

"That'll fuck up your Zagats rating." Gia shivered.

"These are all such ugly fuckers," Max was not wrong. But it did make him wonder why he bothered dressing so well today. If he was going to be the only one putting in any effort at all…

The Angel Metatron put up his hands as his eyes went black. That's how I'm going to start writing stuff for Tim from now on. All pompous and exalted.

"Wait. I've always wanted to say this. I have a message from God."

"Isn't that a line from…"

"Sh. Shut up. Quiet. Be thou silent." He probably didn't say that. I don't know. I'm punchy.

"She says to hold off on killing the demons until she gives the signal. And then kill them all as fast as we can. We have sixty seconds. Or so."

"That seems like an enormous amount of time, thank you." Gia went looking for something that might help. She looked up, "Thank you, God."

"I have never killed anything." Max was not lying. He lived his life as a healer. He once spent half a day chasing a scorpion around an AirBNB in Tempe, Arizona so he could gingerly leave it at a place it could find food, a suitable distance from nearby traffic, out of direct sunlight.

"They are all going to end up back in hell, alive again eventually, anyway. This is all temporary."

"So, temporary kill me some demons?" Max sighed. "I can do that."

As we stepped out of the doorway, A couple of demons hit me square in the chest, . They ripped open my shirt with their black talons and I managed to push them away as the cuts healed.

We were definitely outnumbered. Everyone dove in to fight them. They were all trying to protect me since I had a job to do. Brook stood in front of me and pushed them back. We were keeping them at bay, not killing them. For the first time, I saw Vanessa's eyes go black as she put up some kind of shield to protect us. From what I understand, as long as she was watching out for someone, she was nearly invincible.

The demons threw themselves at the shield, piling up all around it like bales of wheat. Honestly I'm such a city boy that I had to look up that analogy. Originally I was going to say "like trash in the gutter after a street sweeper passes.

Bales of wheat won.

Suddenly a massive roar went up and Onyx colored Jason Momoa stood up in the center of the roof. He cried out.

"Where is she? Where is god?"

Brookly called out, not nearly as loudly, "You mean, in the philosophical sense?"

I pulled out my phone. I looked up. Tim and the others were right above us, floating.

He nodded.

I pressed the button. "Carl. Lock it down."

Strive to Be like the Capybaras

So, we've reached the part of the story where my family spends close to one hundred billion dollars to save Manhattan. I personally think there is a lot more to this story and that everyone else did their part, too, but every time my family discusses it, that is the headline.

Aram family spends 94 billion dollars in crazy day because hijinks.

I understand it. They weren't here. My aunt was on a honeymoon after having eloped two days later as her wedding had turned into a massive shitshow traumatizing her favorite nephew and not incidentally, almost killing one of her best friends and favorite tailor.

Speaking of him, I leaned over the edge of the roof and yelled out to him, "Khalid?"

He looked up, now in fierce battle with what looked like a gigantic cherry flavored snot-like jello shot someone had hawked out of the little cup onto the floor. "Hey, Sunny. How are you?" He seemed unsurprised.

"I'm good. Everything's good. Dimah sends her best."

"That's sweet. I hope the honeymoon is going well." I could tell he did not. Not really.

"Hey, so the plan here right now is kill them all, as fast as you can." This yelling was not good for my voice.

"Kill everything?"

"Yes." I held up two fingers, "We have two minutes."

Khalid began stomping on everything in sight. He put his hand through the Jello Monster and it disappeared.

JelloSnot had a surprise coming.

I turned around and saw the chaos on the rooftop. Vanessa looked at me and put up a shield. I opened wide and screamed, "Get the fuck out of here!"

Hundreds of demons across the rooftop seemed to evaporate and turn to dust, dropping to the ground in waves of blue light and disappearing.

The roof was nearly clear now except for us and the biggest of the three dark demons. He turned to me.

"Where is she?"

I was channeling Brook, "Some of us spend our whole lives looking for God."

He stomped over toward me. He was big. "You are fucking hilarious." He picked me up by the throat.

Suddenly, I realized he was right. I was funny. I was interesting. I could write the hell out of this. The minute we got out of this I would write it all down and I knew just how to start it. Probably with a cool quote. Then, some foreshadowing, writing it after the fact, you know. Get some tension going. I'd be the observing narrator, but also maybe have some omniscient insights into the thinking of the other characters. Brook would be easy to write. We'd been joined at the hip since college and I knew exactly how she thought. Gia would be harder. She's quieter, cooler, harder to figure out. She was like a young Lisa Bonet type character, but just darker and more intense sometimes. This seemed like an awfully weird time to go off on an internal monologue, though, while a demon was trying to choke the shit out of me. I just felt, I dunno, sort of inspired.

The next thing I saw was Brook's sword coming down, removing his arm. I fell to the ground choking. He dropped and rolled, grabbing his amputated arm and swatting her with it. She went flying across the roof.

Vanessa stepped in front of her. I looked around. The demons were all gone on the other rooftops. Gia hovered over the street and gave me a thumbs up. The one armed demon saw what I saw. He must have realized now that most of his legion of little demon guys were now gooey smudges against whatever surface stood between here and hell. No one was coming back.

He reattached his arm and held it in place for a mute until it healed. No lie, that was a good trick. I committed it to memory.

He had to realize he was outnumbered. And by the look in his eyes, he did. He sighed. A wave of resignation crossed his face.

"In for a penny, in for a pound." it seemed to say.

"I Hereby declare my fealty, openly and without reservation - " He began to recite.

Suddenly, a voice rang out across the roof. "I know you."

He turned. Emma stood there, in the green dress she had worn at the wedding. She looked pretty, but small. On her face, though, was a resolve I hadn't seen before. Tim landed behind her and Brooky stepped in next to her. Their eyes glowed black.

"I knew it. I knew you before, when you tried to kill me. But I knew you so much longer ago than that, Jeremiel."

"That's not me, anymore."

"Sure it is. I knew you when you were the only thing I had when Kai died. I knew you when you made me pick up my guitar and sing. Some days, you were the only friend I had. You kept me alive. "

"I'm sorry. But we just want to live, too. These are the rules. You can't be the Godhead." Zeriakl moved in closer. "You're broken. These people below us, they will slit their throats open. You don't even know if you want to live, much less be god."

"You aren't wrong. I'm still working on step two. I don't know what I can outlast. I may just be hanging in there for my friends here." she waved her hands at us. It occurred to me that she never really wanted any of this. And as much as we were leaves in the wind here, so was she. It never hit me that god could be just as powerless as we all were at times. Like prophet Mohammed eunuch level powerless. That will make sense later.

"This is how it has to happen." He advanced on her.

"You're the angel of inspiration. Surely you can see farther than that."

"I wish I... I wish I were."

Emma moved toward him. Her green dress shifted in the dusk and began to glow and change. It softened to a pure white. "What if you help me?"

Zeriakl was lost, "Help you do what?"

She whispered, "break the rules."

She started lifting off the ground with Zeriakl. "My angel of inspiration."

Light bounced from her hands across his body. He closed his eyes.

"Do what you do." Emma's eyes went pure white.

And we could all feel it.

The waves.

And in a nail salon in Soho, a young girl had just finished painting a client's nails with the most perfect tiny cats, little ears rising from the ends like acrylic bumps, so lifelike that you could hear them purr, as a way to prove that she had something inside her - that she was part of god.

And in a food truck sitting in front of a grocery store in Gramercy, an older man placed a row of blackened shrimp over a cream mushroom sauce on top of a red pepper masa tamale, his own recipe, and inhaled one of the most perfect smells that had ever happened on earth in its four billion years, smiling and making his claim to be God.

In a home studio in Brooklyn, Dewonte 17, a local rapper, finished the drums on a track that sounded exactly like he felt on the subway on his way to see his girlfriend, the one he'd been with since grade school, with the ring in his pocket he'd saved up for months, as she texted him a heart and told him that no matter what he was about to ask the answer was yes, a song that would be on the club charts for almost a year and make the case that he should be a part of God.

All over New York, awash in the inspiration wave, people woke up and played, they danced, they painted, they cooked, they made art. And each piece of art rose up and raised its hand. Each one vied to be God.

And in Kigale, Rwanda, Keia, a little girl finished a mural on the wall for the four year old boy, Johari, she babysat, a scene with a massive train carrying every kind of animal you could think of, laughing, nearly falling off the tracks, but held in place by the thick muscular arm of the engine, holding it down. She waited for him to wake up, knowing that he would put his hands over his mouth and smile in joy when he saw it, his dual passions for trains and animals met in creative collision all over his walls, singing out into the broad sky that Keia was indeed God.

And in Guangzhou City in the Guangdong province of China, Yize typed in the last paragraph of his first book, a story about a woman with the same name as his grandmother who had escaped an abusive relationship and gone on to be a world-renowned physicist and teacher, finally dying in her home, surrounded by the students who adored her and promised to carry on her work, a book that he truly believed was the best thing he'd ever done, something beautiful and brilliant and every bit the kind of book someone with a piece of god in him would write.

While, in Jaipur, Rajasthan, nestled in the heart of India, Priyali woke up a full thirty minutes before her alarm, seeing in her head, the exact yarn colors she needed to wrap up her tapestry, the one that showed the procession of elephants where each was a tribute to a family member or loved one, stepping back and viewing the entire thing, alive with the idea that this was better than she was, that it would live longer than she did, that it would be something that even god might find suitable.

And to each of these bids, to every claim, to every single application, Emma softly said, "yes."

All of us on the roof, we could feel it - the waves of inspiration going out. We could feel people changing. We could feel it all.

None of us more than Tim, though.

I reached over and caught him as he fell forward.

"Are you ok, man?"

"It's a lot." He rubbed his eyes. "Every new person I can see what they see. I'm seeing through a million eyes. A billion gods. More."

Vanessa put her hand on his shoulder. "We need to stop this."

Tim grabbed at her, "No, you can't stop. This is working. I'll be ok."

She looked at me, "This is killing him."

"I looked up at Emma holding Zeriakl. Both of them were shaking. He looked like the life was being sucked from him.'

"Emma" I yelled out.

"Don't stop it. Don't you see what she's doing?" Tim held his hands over his eyes, From behind his fists, blood dripped down his cheeks.

"I have to stop it."

Vanessa knelt down to hug him. He forced himself up.

"I can help."

Vanessa held him tightly. "This is killing you."

"Don't you see what she's doing? I'm the voice of god."

Emma looked down, ready to stop. There were tears in her eyes.

He stood up straight and his voice boomed out.

"Don't stop." He dropped his hands. Blood was pouring from his eyes.

Tim looked out for the last time and opened his mouth. It echoed everywhere across the city. It resonated in every head.

"Imago Dei!"

And his eyes exploded out of his head.

It's been two weeks since we fought on the rooftop of the Mongo Motel. We all spent most of that time connecting with people to show them what they could do now. Not all of them. Many people understood innately. Imago Dei.

In the Image of god. Every one of them.

There were billions, after all.

Max was a lot of help. He was the new Jophiel, the angel of beautiful things. He connects with the artists we talk to right away. Long term, he may be the one who nurses new postates along.

Nurses. Get it? I know you should never explain a joke.

"I'm not sure if they're called postates, either." Gia admonished me.

"Uh, I think I'm writing this thing. Do you see the nametag?" There was no nametag.

"Yo mama so fat, she tried to teleport here but the buffer overflowed." Brook looked at me.

I shook my head. "Ok, so there is no buffer on a teleporter, you're thinking of the Star Trek Transporters."

"It's still funny. You're just mad because your momma fat."

Gia looked up, "How come you can teleport with your clothes on but you're always naked when you time travel?"

"Why?" I reached out for my drink.

"Because it's underWHERE, not underWHEN, bitch."

"I drank, "I'm not 100% sure the profanity was necessary on that one."

"It was."

"It really was," Brooky agreed.

"Why did the chicken cross the road?"

"Why, sweetheart?" Brook pet my hands in a special needs affirming way.

"Because he spent ninety four billion dollars in teleporter credits and his family got super pissed and bought him a bicycle."

"Hmm. Little close to home, bikerchicken."

"Too soon?" I took a really long drink.

Tim sat down with a large platter of overfilled drinks the bartender had inexplicably handed to a blind man in the middle of a crowded nightclub. "You know it's like a sixty thousand dollar bike."

"Still hurts."

Vanessa took a drink and toasted, "rich people are weird."

Everyone drank to that. It felt odd to drink it, as well, but it felt odder to abstain.

Giana grabbed a white russian from the platter and lifted it, "To not being dead for some reason."

"Hear hear," Vanessa, the new Cassiel, angel of the downtrodden agreed, her eyes sparkling in the moody club.

"I'm not complaining." Brooky joined in.

"Because I didn't pass on the job. I just shared it." Emma slid into an open chair, with Betina not far behind her. "I figured that work is often lightened with many hands."

"So, she basically said 'yes' to everyone."

I leaned in, "So technically you're still god?"

"I'm still a piece of god. Like so many other people are. I think that this is the way it should have been in the first place. Maybe somebody just got greedy along the way."

Tonight was just an open mic. But later that night she sang three songs and they were good. I'm guessing it would be her name on the front of the club soon, based on the response. It wasn't much, but it was nice to see Emma in her element, just letting go.

Inspired.

Giana was wearing that yellow sundress that made all the guys swoon. It made her skin look so dark and perfect that she could have been an exotic model. And Brooky was in a pair of jeans and a black tank top and guys went crazy over her, too. They didn't even see the best parts.

Me, I do ok with the guys.

Vanessa fed a bird that had just flown in through the window. She talked to it for a few minutes.

"Bye, tweety." Gia took a drink. "You are the most fabulous Disney princess."

"You're going to make me blush.

Later that night, I thought, i would go to my favorite place, this capybara themed cafe I accidentally visited once. And I would sit and write. And I would try to remember the way all this felt, how people looked, what they sounded like.

I would try to remember all of it.

And I would probably think about writing more than I ever had. About what it meant to be a messenger. I'm sure I would get it all wrong and the order I told everything would be completely fucked up. But hopefully some of the people who read it would see my mistakes and their brains would fill it in, making it all better. And maybe they'd understand a little bit of what we went through.

And I guess that's the whole message. I didn't really have a very good ending, but hopefully that would come. It's a nightmare trying to figure out how things come together at the end sometimes.

Vanessa leaned over to whisper to Giana.

"You know, Joan Walsh Anglund has a great quote about why birds sing"

Giana whispered back, "Oh, yeah, what is it?"

The lights dipped and Emma started walking on stage. People applauded and there was energy in the room.

"I'll tell you later- afterward."

Giana picked the cherry out of her drink and threw it at her. "Fucking Tease."

The applause died down as Emma leaned into the mic.

We listened.

And the world didn't really seem all that different.

PANGELICUM

reliquary
ANGELIC

LIBELLUS ANGELORUM

A General Appendix of Angels

ariel

GOD'S TOUCH

POTENS TENEBRAE

azazel
WARRIOR

azrael
ANGEL OF DEATH

INIQUUS UNUS

belial

LAWLESS ONE

cassiel

COMPASSION

JIBREEL

DEI NUNTIUS

gabriel

GOD'S MESSENGER

jeremiel

INSPIRATION

jophiel

GOD'S EYE

kerubiel

PROTECTOR

metatron

DEI VOX

michael

GOD'S WARRIOR

BOBSTAEID MWYROBAS

0 S 0

peabody

GET CLEAN, BITCHES

raguel

JUSTICE

raziel

OF SECRETS

uriel

WISDOM

Brought to you by the people at